Someone Should Save Her

Liars and Vampires, Book 2

Robert J. Crane
With Lauren Harper

Someone Should Save Her
Liars and Vampires, Book 2
Robert J. Crane
with Lauren Harper
Copyright © 2018 Ostiagard Press
All Rights Reserved.

1st Edition

Chapter 1

Where do we begin?

In school, of course. Not in fair Verona, but Tampa—not so fair in winter, when the skies do occasionally go grey and the rains get flipping cold, and the temperature gets close-ish to freezing ...

My name is Cassie Howell, and I'm a compulsive liar.

The weather was definitely the worst that I had seen since moving down to Florida from the snowy rolling hills of New York State. It had been so cold that most of the native Floridians had come to school bundled up in bubble jackets, hats, and gloves. All I'd heard the last week was how cold it had been, how they missed the triple digit temperatures, and how some of them even thought they had seen frost(!) on the grass that morning instead of dew or the remnants from the sprinkler system.

I, on the other hand, was almost comfortable in a sweatshirt and sneakers. I was in *Florida*, for Pete's sake. These yahoos had no idea what cold actually was. They hadn't lived in a place where it didn't matter if it snowed six feet overnight; we still had to go to school.

But that wasn't the only way I was different from all of the other students. No, I was more different than most of them even knew. I was the new girl, sure, but I probably knew something about the city of Tampa and its surrounding neighborhoods that no one else in this class did.

Well, except for Alexandra. Xandra, for short. She hated

being called Alexandra.

Aside from her, no one else in my class knew that I had met—and killed—vampires.

About a month after Christmas, not long after I had moved to Florida with my parents, I'd met Byron, a handsome, conceited boy who claimed to go to my school. It was very quickly evident that he did not. After he cornered Xandra and me in her dad's business one night, an entire world of vampires opened up before me.

I had attended a vampire soirée, been visited by vampires, and had had a showdown with Byron in his own home, where I outsmarted and eventually killed him. Self-defense, just FYI, no murder for funsies here. If killing the undead still counted as murder, at any rate.

That was three months ago. Since then, my life had pretty much gone back to normal, thank God. I was going to all of my after-school activities, including math league. Now that I was back on a healthy sleeping schedule, my grades were on the rise, and I was being a good girl, following all of the rules.

Things with Mom and Dad were polite, if a bit tense. I think Mom felt sorry for me, which I took in stride—pity was way preferable than anger and snide remarks. Dad had been extra nice as of late, making my favorite dishes for dinner on the weekends, buying me a new laptop, and even offering to get me my own car once I got my driver's license. Which I was behind on getting due to the move.

We had sort of agreed without saying it that we were not going to bring up Byron, and how he had stalked me and then kidnapped them. Which probably wasn't the best approach for them—they didn't know that Byron was dead. I think they secretly believed he was going to pop back up in our lives. But for me, every day that passed without us talking about it was a good day. The most important change since then: I was doing everything I could to avoid the lies that had caused me so much trouble in the first place.

Except … yeah. My lying days weren't quite done yet.

It was a Thursday, and I was sitting in my sixth period class, English. Yet again, we were working through a

Chapter 2

"Vampires," I said coolly, my hands going to my hips.

Though class was in session, a few students were milling about the halls. Threatened by possibly being overheard, Gregory hissed at me, grappled me by the arm and dragged me around the next, deserted corner.

"Hey!" I said.

"Keep your voice down!" he whispered.

"Keep my—*you said it in the first place*," I hissed.

"Not as loud as you did!"

I pursed my lips—part irritation, part to lock out the underlying scent of Pine-Sol, which smelled more like bathroom than Christmas tree and pervaded the school in an unpleasant fog. I swear it was getting worse lately.

Gregory swallowed hard. In a whisper, he said, "Someone I know is being stalked by ... by one," he settled on. "Or more than one. I don't know. I just know—" He looked all around, but we were still totally alone. "It's a vampire."

"How do you *know* that?" I asked.

He looked around again, rubbing his hand over the nape of his neck. His hair still clung to his forehead. "They're coming after her at night. *Only* at night." Gregory wasn't easily flustered. It gave my disbelief pause. He'd admitted to me, without shame and straight to my face, that he'd been watching me through his window, as if it were the most normal thing in the world. So to see him like this, so het up ... I couldn't deny that something was very seriously the

7

matter here.

Still, I said, "That doesn't mean anything. They could just be night owls, or maybe they have the night shift or something. Or maybe they're college students. People in college never sleep, right?"

Gregory didn't seem to think anything I was saying was funny.

"And why are you saying, 'they'? What's up with the pronoun game? Is this a Tumblr thing?"

Gregory whispered, "I think it might be more than one person."

"Might?" I asked. "So you aren't even sure?"

He pursed his lips together and sighed heavily through his nose, dropping his eyes to the floor.

"Look, I don't know what to think or say, okay?" he said, desperation clearly written all over his face.

"All right, chill out," I said, a prick of worry creeping into my mind. "There are a ton of explanations for why this could be happening. Vampires don't have to be the definite go-to."

Gregory turned to look at me again.

"I mean, I hate to say it, but what if this person you know has a stalker? Or a jealous ex? Or something that is way more reasonable than a vampire?"

Gregory hung his head but stayed silent.

"Listen, classes are about to get out—"

"They're vampires. I know it," Gregory finally said. He spoke with absolute certainty—and despite trying to convince him that he was incorrect, that there was a perfectly rational explanation for what he had seen, I felt the blood drain out of my face at the possibility that he was correct. "Cassie, please," he said, laying a hand on my shoulder. "Can you help?"

I brushed his hand away. "Let me put it to you the way you did to me just a couple of months ago ... um, no."

He shook his head slightly, maybe trying to clear some of the insanity that seemed to have taken root. "Wait, why not?"

"Because I'm out," I said, taking a step backward from him, my hands up in the air in surrender. "Done. Kaput.

it—and Gregory's crestfallen face, echoing in my mind, was not going to convince me otherwise.

"What was that about?"

Fortunately I had expected Xandra to show up, because if I hadn't, I probably would have reflexively whacked her in the face with my heavy psych textbook.

I glanced at her briefly before checking to make sure that the other girl a few down from me had walked away.

"*Vampires*," I mouthed. No one could care less about what two girls were talking about next to their lockers, but I still didn't want to draw any attention.

Xandra's aquamarine eyes grew wide. "I thought we were past all that." She shifted her own stack of books in her arms.

"Not my problem this time," I said, closing my locker with more force than was probably necessary. "It's really not."

Was I trying to convince her? Or myself?

"I thought that if you got tangled up with the vamps again …" Xandra said softly, also looking around for unwanted eavesdroppers. There were none. "Didn't Iona warn you?"

Iona was one of the vampires who had not tried to kill me. An eternal photograph of an emo teen, she had been nice, if somewhat infuriating to deal with on the other end of a text message. Her advice had been extremely useful, even if it had led me into the depths of a vampire party.

The stake she'd given me to defend myself with had been even better.

The last time I had seen her was just days after beating Byron, when she had turned up at school and warned me that if I got involved with the vamps of Tampa again, I risked exposing my actual identity to Lord Draven, the vampire ruler of the city—another very good reason for me *not* to jump headlong into Laura Grayson's apparent vampire problem.

"Yes," I replied. "She did. And trust me, the last thing that I want is to cross … *him*," I said. Xandra knew perfectly well who I was talking about.

I was terrified of doing that, if I was honest. Really terrified. I had looked him in the eye and lied, point blank, pretending to be a vampire. And he had bought it.

"He still thinks that you're a ... y'know ..." Xandra said under her breath as we walked beside each other going down the stairs to the first floor. "From a different state? Like that you aren't around anymore?"

"Well, if he knew that I wasn't what I said I was, then I probably *wouldn't* be around anymore, would I?"

Xandra's face paled, but she nodded.

"Yeah ... that wouldn't be good."

Understatement. Blood and chaos. Unbridled fear. Draven's wrath, as I understood it, would be way worse than anything that Shakespeare could have ever come up with.

"So are these ... people ... bothering Gregory?"

I shook my head. I brushed a stray curl out of my face, finding that any tiny thing out of place right now was almost intolerable.

I didn't feel right sharing Laura's name. Xandra thought Laura Grayson was the worst thing to ever show up in her life. I figured Xandra, like the rest of us, was jealous of Laura, and of all of the attention she got. But I didn't feel like dealing with her complaining about Laura, so I just shook my head. "Not him, no. It's someone he knows."

Xandra chewed on her bottom lip. "Do you think that it actually is vampires? Maybe one of the ones you know?"

I sighed. "I have no idea. But Gregory says they're only showing up at night, so ... maybe."

"But that doesn't mean ..."

"That's exactly what I said!" I snapped. A little more graciously, I added, "You're right, it doesn't. But he was so afraid ..."

We walked into our Psychology class and found our seats toward the back of the room. Psych was one of my favorite classes. I enjoyed learning about how the mind worked and why people thought the way they did about different things. And for the last two months, I'd had straight As.

"So what are you going to do?" Xandra asked over my shoulder.

It should have been easy to reply. Of course I was going to stay out of it. I'd almost lost my life because vampires had enjoyed doing *normal* things.

Then again, I figure anyone would after crossing paths with vampires. Nothing like a threat to your life—and your parents'—by something from a Bram Stoker novel to impress on you the value of the mundane.

"Thank you for taking care of those," she said finally. "It's a big help. *You've* been a big help. Your father and I appreciate it."

I shrugged my shoulders. "No biggie."

Silence fell as we cleaned up after dinner, and I put the rest of the chicken on a plate for Dad to heat up when he got home.

"Hey, Mom? Would it be okay if I went up to my room and watched some Netflix? I'm exhausted."

She had no idea. The conversation with Gregory was filling my brain to the maximum, and I needed some space from it all.

"Did you finish all of your homework?"

"Yep."

"I know you did the chores down here, but did you finish cleaning up all of the makeup in your bathroom?"

"Before I left this morning."

She nodded.

Even though she was starting to trust me, she was looking for a reason to say no to me. I could understand why, I really could.

"Did you want me to check your math for you?" she asked. "I know you were complaining about it last night."

I handed her my notebook without a word—even if this was just another way of checking on me.

But how could I blame her? It was my fault that our relationship had come to this. And I wanted her to be able to trust me. After all of the lying ...

I wanted a normal life. I wanted that connection with my parents, no matter how tough it was some days, feeling the doubt coming off her every question, nearly every word.

She skimmed through the problems. "Looks like you finally got it," she said. I appreciated the falsely positive attitude, because I know she didn't want to be outright accusatory.

"I did," I said. "Thanks for your help last night."

Mom looked at me again, tapping her fingers on her arms. She finally shrugged.

"All right, if you want to go relax for a while, I don't see any problem with it."

Relieved, I grabbed my bag, thanked her, and retreated to my room.

I was almost giddy as I slid under my covers in my bed with my earbuds and phone, plugged firmly in to charger. The tension of the day had been steadily creeping up my neck again. A cool pillow to the back of it was definitely the tonic I needed.

Netflix app open, I scanned through show title cards, wondering which I wanted to watch. Two less than stellar recommendations greeted me, almost at the very top: *Vampire Diaries* and *Vampire Knights*. I scowled at them and slid on past.

I still had a few episodes of *Pretty Little Liars* to catch up on, so I picked that. Getting lost in someone else's drama for a while seemed like a nice way to pass the time.

I was just about to put my earbuds in when I heard something crash outside.

Instantly, my heart was thudding against my chest. Unbidden, visions of Byron rose instantly in my mind: him having ripped through the fence, grappling Mom, an arm thrown around her chest, the other angling her head back as she screamed, and he grinned at me in that manic way, fangs glinting as he lowered them to her neck—

Swallowing back my fear, I clambered out of bed on heavy legs, parted the curtains and looked outside.

It was dark, but there was plenty of illumination from the street lights. Two doors down, just past Gregory's house, I saw people standing in the yard.

Was that ... Laura Grayson's house?

The little hairs at the back of my neck stood up straight. I pulled open the blinds a little and cracked the window.

They were a rowdy bunch, their voices reaching all the way up to my room as soon as I let the night in.

There were four of them, and they looked like a bunch of

incredibly strong, and if I was honest with myself, it was sheer dumb luck that had saved me both times I had fought them before.

If I were to go into a fight with these vampires head on, then I would end up as dinner.

Even so, there had to be a way to get them to leave.

I pulled my phone from my pocket and opened my contacts list. I scrolled through until I found Iona's name.

It had been three months since I had spoken to her, and I had been perfectly fine with that. But she was the only one that I knew who might be able to help.

Any advice on scaring off vampires? I texted. **Got a bunch in my neighborhood, causing mischief.**

I hit send, hoping that I'd get an answer soon. Like in the next minute soon.

Knowing I shouldn't waste my time, I looked around, trying to assess what I could use to my advantage.

A whole lot of nothing.

Grass. A hose. Maybe I could spray holy water at them through the hose?

Hah. Nice thought, and a sort of funny image, but that was never going to happen. I'd have to bless the garden tap, for starters, if not the mains delivering the water in the first place—and a priest, I was not. Something to look into for later. Maybe I should look into befriending a priest at the very least, based on how often I was running into vamps these days.

I continued my visual search over the yard. Shovels. Rakes. Useless to me. I would lose the fight with those as soon as I started it.

I was starting to get desperate.

My phone buzzed in my hand, and I opened it quickly, hungrily.

They'll run when the cops get there.

My brow furrowed as I stared at the screen. I double-checked the name at the top of the message. No, it was definitely Iona.

Was she crazy?

I looked up, hearing the group two doors down dump

25

something else over in the yard, followed by more laughter. There couldn't be much more yard left for them to destroy.

What was the likelihood that someone in this oh-so-nice, picture perfect, American dream sort of neighborhood would call the cops?

I chewed on my lip. **Why?** I sent back in reply.

Her response came within a second. **DRAVEN**.

I wasn't sure why I didn't see it before. Of course they would run. If they caused enough mayhem to bring the cops down, they'd have to answer to Draven, the vampire Lord of the territory. And if my meeting him had made me see anything about him, it was that he liked his territory neat and tidy, off the radar of the humans. He wouldn't want trouble with the law.

Therefore, the squad of vamps less than two hundred yards away would flee when the cops came rolling down the street.

Feeling the blood thud in my eardrum, I keyed in 9-1-1, and was just about to press dial when—sirens wailed in the distance.

Someone had alerted the police first.

"Looks like the party's over for now!" one of the vampires shouted up at Laura's window as red and blue lights strobed across the edges of her house from the street—the police car had pulled to a stop at her curb. "Don't worry, Laura. We will be back for you soon!"

More cackles, taunts for her to come out to them, and then they turn to scatter just as car doors closing echoed in the night.

Thing was—where were they scattering *to*?

Gregory's yard first, vaulting the fence in perfectly graceful leaps—

And then, I realized as a wave of ice overflowed—they surged for mine.

I had less than a second to make a decision. They hadn't seen me yet. Throwing myself down as quick as a flash, I rolled underneath the bushes bordering the fence, breath held—

The vampires landed barely inches from where I'd just been standing. For all the noise they'd been making, hollering up at

Laura, it was almost easy to forget how unnaturally graceful they were. Their landings were near-silent—ridiculous for creatures who were about as hard as concrete, and just as strong.

My breath burned in my chest. My heart thudded, triple-time.

This was the closest I had been to vampires in months—and unlike the party Iona had sent me to, I had never felt more vulnerable. Pressed to the dirt, the earthy scent filling my nostrils even though I didn't dare breathe, thorns and jagged branches pressing into my skin, I was effectively defenseless. I had my stake, sure—but I lay prone, unable to reach it if they heard me and turned.

And they would hear me. They'd pick up the sound of my frenzied heartbeat in an instant—if they were looking for it.

Four pairs of legs crossed the yard—away.

I didn't dare breathe. Didn't dare move. Just stared, out of the corner of one panicked eye, at their receding backs, moving silently through the night, to the edge of the house, then around it—and into darkness.

Then, and only then, did I permit myself to refill my lungs.

It took me a moment or two to pull myself out from underneath the bush once I was convinced that they were truly gone. The lights from the police car still strobed the night, casting long, menacing shadows around the yard. Thankful for the flashlight on my cell, I opened it, and convinced that I was alone in the yard, started back inside the lanai.

I was torn. In one sense, I was somewhat proud of myself for leaping into action, ready to do what I could. Another part of me, though, felt pretty useless. Realistically, what *could* I do? The cops had been my best bet, and I hadn't even pulled the trigger on that myself.

I sighed as I pulled a twig from my hair, putting my hand on the doorknob to go back inside. Whether I knew how to help or not, the choice was clear. I was already in over my head and had been since the beginning. The past few months had been nice—but they were a reprieve from this vampire problem, and only that. A short break, time enough to draw a breath, to remember what life was like before a life was in peril. Last time it was mine ... this time, Laura's. Either way ...

I was in.

Chapter 6

I stepped back into the kitchen and came face to face with my mother.

"What is going on out there?" she asked, her hand over her chest. "And what in the world were you doing? I didn't even see you leave."

"Oh," I said, and decided to go with mostly the truth. "I heard some noises and looked outside. There was some kind of crazy gang, or a group of drunk teenagers, that were raising all kinds of hell two doors down."

Her face showed that that was not what she had expected me to say. "How terrible," she said quietly. She rolled her shoulders, fighting back tension.

"Between things like this," she said, gesturing back out the door that I had come through, "and what happened a few months ago—" there was no need to specify which event she was referring to "—I'm starting to wonder if this was the best neighborhood for us to have moved to." She muttered about the research she and Dad had done into the location ... then, snapping from her thoughts, she said,

"Are you all right?"

I nodded. "Fine."

"You look like you were on the ground."

"I was," I replied, still attempting to stick with the honesty as far as I could stretch it. "I didn't want them to see me."

She glared. "Why would you go outside to look? That's insane."

"I just wanted to make sure that my friend was okay," I said. "Gregory Holt was shouting out his window at them." I clicked my tongue in annoyance. "Idiot."

"No kidding," Mom said. "Did I see a police car pull up?"

I nodded again. "I guess someone called them. I was about to when it pulled up."

"Well," Mom said heavily, shaking her head. "Are they gone now?"

"Yeah, they took off."

"I hope the police catch them."

"Me too," I said, relishing the idea of Draven killing those four on the spot for disturbing the peace. Four fewer vampires in the world would do it a lot of good. I hated Draven, but if any sort of connection to me could be eliminated, the better off I would be.

"I'm going to call to your father," Mom said finally. "Stay inside, okay? I don't want you out there. Though I suppose the police may want you as a witness if you saw anything ..." She trailed off.

"If you need me, or they show up, I'll be in my room," I said. "I didn't really see much, though."

Mom nodded, lost in her own thoughts.

I fell back into my bed, pulling my headphones off of the bedside table again, and plugging my phone charger in. Trying to throw myself into normal life once again, I started up the episode of *Pretty Little Liars* I had been about to watch before being so rudely interrupted.

But five minutes in, I couldn't focus. All I could think about was Laura.

How long had she been plagued like this? Obviously a while—Gregory had seen it at least once before tonight, and the vampires knew her name. They had chosen her for some reason. It hadn't taken Byron very long to lay claim to me, at least in his mind. I knew what that was like.

I felt bad for Laura, I really did. No one would understand what she was going through like I did. But what could I do? It wasn't like I could have single-handedly driven them away tonight. And what if they came back and bothered Laura when I wasn't around, or couldn't help?

Unless I moved in with the girl and handcuffed us together, I wasn't likely to experience all of their visits.

It irked me that I couldn't see a solution but wanted to. I wanted there to be a way out of this for her—not least, I recognized with a stab of guilt, because it would allow me to move on too. Around and around I went, wondering at questions with no answers. *Pretty Little Liars* started and ended in front of me, no more than background noise. Finally, the red and blue lights flashing in through my window, and the still-open curtains, faded away as the squad car left.

Grateful that the police hadn't knocked on our door to ask for statements, and also hoping that they'd found something that would lead them to the vamps, I tried to relax into my blankets.

It was no good. All of the exhaustion seemed to have left my body, and both my mind and my muscles were awake. I could have run a marathon right then if I had wanted to. Part of me considered it.

But Mom had asked me to stay inside, and I fully intended on following her orders. What would I see out there, anyway?

All I could think was that Laura, Gregory, and I were the only ones who really knew the truth. And something told me that they wouldn't spill the beans to anyone else.

Just as I felt my eyelids beginning to droop, there was a quiet, gentle tapping at my window.

Chapter 7

A girl not far from my age, with sad, unblinking eyes, perched on the sill outside.

"Iona," I breathed, and crossed to throw the window open without thinking. Bad move, I'd think later—inviting a vampire into your house had gone horribly, terribly wrong for me once already—but Iona was a friend, if an infuriatingly vague one at times.

A strong smell of roses and fresh pine washed in with the cool air as she slid gracefully into the room. Her silvery blond hair fell like a waterfall over her shoulders, all the way down her back. She straightened, her stance like a cat's, and she turned to face me, brushing some stray hair from her bright, amber eyes.

"Come on in," I said, obviously as an afterthought.

She blinked at me. "I apologize for barging in like this," she began, her voice cool and even like a mountain lake. "But given what has happened in your little neighborhood in the last few days, a conversation up on the rooftop or out in public isn't really a great option. It will draw the wrong kind of attention."

"I'm a little surprised to see you, to be honest," I said, flopping down on my bed, my headphones still in my hand.

"You were the one asking for advice about how to get rid of vampires."

"Well, yeah, but whatever happened to texting me?"

Iona crossed her arms over her chest, her leather jacket

catching the light from my bedside table lamp. "Did you think that vampires reappearing in your area would fail to get my attention?"

"Well, no—"

"So I came right over. The last time I hesitated, Byron ended up kidnapping your parents." There was a low note of remorse in her voice—very low; the barest trace of guilt.

"I'm also concerned these vampires might be Draven's men."

"Well, it wasn't exactly men," I said. "And they weren't exactly old, either."

"What do you mean?" Iona asked, her brow furrowing.

"There were four of them, but they all looked like they could have been in my year at school. And they were acting really odd, too." "Odd," of course, meaning nothing like Byron—because I didn't exactly know how vampires acted in general. Of course, with Draven's desire to keep in the shadows, I figured it was fair to say that vamp hoodlums disturbing the neighborhood wasn't exactly par for the course.

I gave Iona a quick rundown of what happened. I told her about how I had heard them and how they had nearly burned down the entire neighborhood. I told her that I had watched as they had carried on and taken pictures, and how they had run, just as she had said, when the police were called.

"And they must have attracted more attention than they had thought, because it wasn't me that had called the cops. Someone beat me to it."

Iona nodded.

"So why do you think that these four are harassing you?"

It took me a second to register what she had said. "Wait," I said. "I think you have the wrong impression. They aren't harassing me. They're after this girl in my class, my neighbor."

Her nostrils flared with annoyance. "Why didn't you say that from the beginning?"

"I'm sorry," I replied. "Her name is Laura. She's the head cheerleader at my school. Tall, pretty, the top of the class—a total walking cliché if ever there was one." I paused. Acid had crept into my voice.

"All right, that wasn't so nice."

Iona's gaze had never left my face. "What did this girl do to you?"

I had to think. "Well, nothing, really. I don't know."

"Then why do you hate her?"

"Hate her?" I said, my head spinning a little. "I don't hate her. She's been … nice to me, I guess."

Iona arched a perfectly tweezed eyebrow. "Are you sure? It sounds like—"

"I'm sure," I cut in. "She's nice, really. She's popular, everyone likes her. She's—" I hesitated. "Never mind. Maybe envy wasn't a thing when you were growing up."

Iona cracked a smile. A smile! I wasn't sure I had ever seen that sort of look on her face.

"I'm not that much older than you," Iona said.

"I know that," I replied. "But how long have you been nineteen or whatever?"

Iona looked at her black Converse shoes with the dirty white laces.

No answer, so I heaved a sigh. "I thought that all of this was behind me, you know?"

"I thought so too," Iona said.

"And then, after all this time, they somehow show up again in my neighborhood, harassing one of my classmates! I mean, what are the chances of that?"

Iona nodded.

"I thought that when Gregory came to me blabbing about vampires that he was blowing something way out of proportion, that maybe he was just upset that someone else was after his crush. But I just didn't want to think about it. I mean, he had only seen Byron. He wasn't there when I had to actually face them … the coward."

Iona's eyes narrowed. "Someone else knows about us?"

I waved her statement away. "Don't act so surprised."

Iona's eyebrows nearly reached her scalp, but I ignored it.

"But this girl, Laura," I started again, grabbing a pillow and draping it across my knees before leaning my elbows on it, "she has no idea what she's up against. I've been there. I know exactly what she is feeling. How can I just leave her to deal with these vamps?"

Iona drummed her fingers against her arm, but I spoke again before she opened her mouth.

"It's not that I want to get involved. That is literally the last thing in the entire world that I want. I've spent the last three months trying to get my life back to normal. It's not like I've had nightmares almost every night since all of this started, or like I've had the absolute worst time trying to get my parents to trust me again. I have so much to lose if I even consider getting involved."

I sighed, my eyes falling on the little unicorn statuette that Byron had picked up and examined one of the last times he had been in my room. For some reason I hadn't gotten rid of it yet, in spite of the dread-inducing memories it inspired in me. Defiance, maybe—one last middle finger to Byron.

"But I still worry about her, and what could happen to her. I mean, if I don't step in, she could be killed. And I have the knowledge to help her, have the experience. That was why Gregory came to me."

I sighed and fell back onto the bed.

"I don't know, Iona," I said. I didn't try to hide the defeat in my voice. "I just can't help thinking that I should help."

She finally broke in. "Because someone is clearly in over their head?"

I glared at her. "What? Her or me?"

"Both of you," Iona replied flatly. She crossed the room in two steps and was seated beside me before I had even blinked. "You should stay out of this, Cassie. Remember, Lord Draven is looking for you. Even if these four hooligans weren't sent by him, they're in his territory. That means they answer to him. If he finds you—"

"Yeah, I know," I said. "All of my blood, drained from my body, and not for a good cause like saving cancer patients."

Iona rolled her eyes.

"But theoretically," I said, "If I did want to help ... what could I do?"

Iona rose to her feet in one fluid motion. It wasn't fair, how graceful she was. But her gaze turned on me was all ice.

"Call the police the next time you see them, or hear them

coming," she suggested, not gently. "That's the best thing that you can do—spook them."

She put her hands on her hips and stared intently down at me. "Don't get involved, Cassandra. You won't survive it."

And without another word, leaving me both reeling and angry all at the same time, she vanished out the window like a bird making for freedom. The wind rushed in after her, as if to punctuate her exit.

"You don't have to be so dramatic about it," I muttered under my breath before collapsing back onto my blankets again.

Chapter 8

No sooner had I closed my eyes, it seemed, than the night was over, vanquished with the shrill bleat of my alarm.

Mom was waiting for me downstairs, and I only half heard her telling me about what the plans for the weekend were. It wasn't until I was waving at her as I walked into the school, travel mug full of chocolate milk and coffee in hand, that I realized that it was Friday.

Not that Friday really meant all that much to me these days. I liked being able to sleep in on Saturdays, but what teenager didn't? I was just putting my backpack inside my locker when—

"Hey, Cassie."

Rubbing sleep from my eyes, I turned to find Gregory behind me, smelling of a cologne that made me think of beaches and free time. Wearing a plaid shirt today and dark blue jeans—a look that suited him, I noted with some annoyance—he looked tired, green eyes underlined with dark circles under his glasses.

"Did you see what happened last night?" he asked, voice low and eyes flitting to see if anyone was watching us. They weren't; no one cared what us zeroes were discussing.

I closed my locker and leaned against it. "It was kinda hard to miss. I mean, someone called the police."

"Wait, that *wasn't* you?" he said. He pushed his glasses up his nose before running his fingers through his hair.

"No," I said. "But I'd recommend that you guys switch to

a charcoal grill, for safety's sake. Or maybe even get rid of a grill altogether. Otherwise you've got a potential bomb in your yard for a vampire to set off if they get pissed at you again." *Or just decide it's fun,* I didn't add.

"This isn't a joke," Gregory said harshly, all of the color draining from his face.

I stared coolly back at him, unfazed. "You're right. Vampires came after you last night. Explosions, or permanent hearing loss would be the least of your—"

Face contorting with anger at my flippancy, Gregory spun around on the spot and, avoiding a group of giggling freshmen, paced across the hall. He looked up and down the hall, and then walked back to me.

"I didn't sleep at all last night," he said, looking around again for eavesdroppers.

"I'm sorry," I said. I remembered what that felt like. "I get it. Things are a little tense right now—"

"A *little*?" Gregory ran an anxious hand through his hair.

"You're gonna have to calm down, buddy," I told him. "No one would normally care what we're talking about, but you're drawing attention to us."

And he was. Several pairs of eyes nearby had fixed themselves upon us—on *him*. Drawn back to reality, he straightened, adjusting his grip on his books—back to business-as-usual Gregory Holt, not totally-freaking-out-right-now Gregory.

Gawkers returning to their lockers and conversation, I said, "Look, I *am* taking this seriously."

I had spent most of the night after Iona left going back and forth in my mind. Iona's advice was solid, and it didn't take an idiot to know that heeding her was the best way to keep myself safe. There was nothing saying that I had to get involved.

But my conscience was nagging me relentlessly, and it wasn't until I stood there in front of Gregory that I realized I had made my decision a long time ago.

"And ..." I continued, "I'm ready to help."

Relief washed over Gregory's face as his eyes widened and the color returned to his cheeks. "Really? For real? For really real?"

I could only blink at him. "Can we just go with yes?"

"Okay," he said, and it was as if a weight had left his shoulders. He looked nervously around, and before I could say anything, he snaked his hand around my elbow and started to steer me down the hall.

"Hey," I said, trying to pull away, "what are you doing?"

"Come with me," he said. "Please."

The fear was back in his voice, and so I complied.

He led me down the hall, and we took a right turn down the English hallway. Laura stood at her locker, staring inside, rearranging books and surrounded by her friends.

Gregory halted our steps.

"Why aren't we going to talk to her?" I asked.

"Look," Gregory said.

So I looked. She was laughing at something that one of the senior boys had said to her, his letterman's jacket draped over his arm. All of the girls were gazing at her in awe, and all of the guys were looking at her as if they were staring at an angel.

But Laura was struggling. Maybe it wasn't obvious to all of her admirers swarming around her like bees to honey, but I knew what to look for. Her smile didn't quite reach her eyes, where dark circles were covered by a thick layer of foundation. Her books were nestled right in front of her chest, creating a barrier between her and all of those other students surrounding her. And her perfect curls seemed as if a little less time had been put into them that morning. Everyone had mornings where they slept in, right?

Not Laura Grayson.

"She's not even talking about what happened to her last night," Gregory said, bending down to my ear. "Can you believe it? Vampires practically put her house under siege and she's listening that girl talk about her hair care woes."

"Maybe she realizes that telling the truth would make her sound completely insane." Again, I could sympathize.

Gregory's eyes stayed on her with intensity that bordered on adoration. "This girl is different than you. If she told them that there were vampires after her, everyone would believe her."

That stung. This girl was different than me. So what? It wasn't like I wanted people to fawn over me like a bunch of idiots, hanging on my every word, as if I was a goddess or some kind of prophet.

Acidly, I snapped, "Yeah, right." I crossed my arms over my chest, biting down on my tongue, my face hardening into stone.

Gregory caught his mistake a moment too late.

"I ..." he started. "I didn't mean it like that."

"Whatever." The perpetual retort of the scorned teenage girl. If I hadn't been so wounded by what he'd said, maybe I would have put more original thought into it.

The bell rang through the crowded hall—five minutes until homeroom. Corridors were starting to clear out now, Laura's friends moving off with short goodbyes. Between that and the fact that our loitering, and staring, was increasingly obvious the longer we dallied (a fact which probably didn't bother Gregory, considering his total lack of shame), he took a chance:

"Hey, Laura?"

Laura turned from her locker.

"Hi, Gregory," she said, her face lighting up.

So it wasn't all just a ruse. She seemed genuinely pleased to see him. Then again, she always looked genuinely pleased to see everyone. But there was a sort of giddiness when she saw him, as if he was an answer to a prayer.

Gregory took the greeting as an invitation to practically skip up alongside her—and pull me along by my elbow in his wake, spluttering. "Laura, this is Cassie Howell."

"I know Cassie," she said, smiling at me.

Tearstains on the front of her blouse, I noticed—faded, because they'd almost dried, saltwater spreading into blurred smears. But I noticed them, even if her friends hadn't. After last night, the fact that she was trying to carry on normally was admirable.

Just like everything she else she did.

"She lives right beside me," Gregory continued.

"Yeah, we share yards," I added.

Laura's smile faltered. The color faded from her cheeks. A frantic glance between us, unmasked—and then she turned back to her locker, digging in it for books as though she were arms-deep in Mary Poppins' bag.

"So I guess you heard the craziness at my house last night?" she asked, her casual tone not very well faked. She covered with an over-hearty laugh. "I'm really sorry. Some friends just got ... out of control, I guess." She sounded dead inside, like a woman covering for an abuser, or someone trying to explain why Coldplay was actually good.

I decided to not beat around the bush. Not this time. Not with three minutes until homeroom. My record had been spotless since January.

"And here I thought that you had vampire stalkers." I shrugged, my hands in my pockets. "Color me embarrassed if they're just a bunch of losers of the garden variety."

Laura's face fell as she stared back at me—and then she laughed, shaking her head. "Oh, right. Funny." Her eyes popped a little as she made spooky fingers with her hands. "*Vampires*. Right."

"It's okay," I said, and reached across to her, placing my hand on her shoulder. "I had one too. A really bad one." I had to admit that it was odd to be talking about the vampires so frankly in school. And with someone other than Xandra.

Both Laura and Gregory visibly stiffened.

The two of them exchanged glances, a silent conversation passing between them:

Can we trust her?

Laura bit down on her lip. "How ... how did it turn out?"

There was the admission of truth. There was no backing out now. She knew that I knew, and she had admitted it.

How much better off she was already than I had been.

"He ... kidnapped my parents," I said, getting right to the worst of it. There was no sense in mincing words with the poor girl. "And I kind of ... staked him."

Laura's eyes grew wide, and I heard Gregory exhale in admiration behind me.

"Wow ..." she said. "How?"

"It's a long story."

"What do they want from me?" She was almost whispering now.

"Hard to say for sure, but from my point of view it seems like they want you to join them in their YOLO lifestyle, dead or alive. Or undead. However that works."

She swallowed hard, drawing her arms in closer to herself. "They ... keep taking pictures. Like, posing for selfies. It's how I met them."

"Were you alone?" I asked.

She nodded. "I was at the mall, looking for a prom dress. They were in Macy's too, and just came right up to me, cell phones out and ready. The ring leader, the girl, was like, 'You're pretty. Bet you'd increase our follower count.'"

"Did you ... take photos with them?" I asked. I felt a perverse sense of déjà vu as I remembered opening the window for Byron the first time. As though letting them take a picture with you was tantamount to inviting them into your house. Laura shrugged, eyes glued to the tiled floor. "I didn't see the harm in it. I mean, kids in school ask to take their picture with me all the time."

It took everything in me not to roll my eyes. She didn't need that right now. I was being Emotional Support Cassie. To Laura Grayson. Argh.

"They were ... intense, and very awkward," she continued.

"I'm just gonna ask this," I tossed out there, "because it's bugging me. Why does their follower count matter?"

Gregory pushed his glasses up his nose. "Why does the score matter in a video game?" Laura and I both gave him a pitying look, but he was not fazed, looking between us like we were the idiots.

"Because it's a metric you use to keep score in life," he explained. "That's their follower count. It's their determination of if they're *winning*."

"Winning what?" I asked. "Are there cash prizes for this? Did I miss something? Is this a viable living now, taking pictures of yourself on the internet?" I cleared my throat. "Of, the, uh ... non-naughty variety?"

"For some people, getting likes on their photos means everything to them," Laura said. "One girl took eighty selfies

42

before she posted one she liked. Eighty."

"That is really sad," I said. "You die, and in your afterlife, you're still stuck giving a damn if people like you. Instaphoto is like high school forever." I shook my head. "It sounds a little like hell to me."

"It's not that bad," Laura replied. "I have an account."

"Oh," I said. "Did I say hell? I meant of the, uhm ... not ... burning everything variety."

Her eyes lit up as she pulled her phone out of her pocket. "I mean, there are some great accounts to follow. Some cheerleading ones, those are totally critical. A daily meditation account that reminds me to be mindful, and they post from some of the most unbelievable places—"

"You should find one that teaches you to kill vampire stalkers," I said.

She paused, suddenly thoughtful. "You know ... I bet there's one out there like that. I'll see if I can find it."

I looked around at the now empty hallway. Homeroom was coming up fast, as evidenced by people running by.

"What are you going to do?" Laura asked, eyes on the prize—or at least me.

"Me?" I asked, and she nodded. "I'm probably going to consult with my source in the vampire world ... and find out who these people are."

"Then what?" she asked, her eyes widening. "Have a nice chat over some warmed-over O negative non-fat lattes with nutmeg?"

Gregory grinned. "That's a good one."

I glared at him, but had to concede it was pretty good.

I bit down on the inside of my lip and stared at a dent in Laura's locker door.

I had to make sure that Laura really understood the situation she was in. She was scared, yes, but I wasn't really sure that she was aware that her life was on the line. Not really.

"These vampires," I began slowly. "They intend to *kill* you, Laura. And that means the only way to stop them is to either scare them off ... which I don't know if it's possible in the long-term ... or ..."

I had to take a deep breath and push the faces of both Byron and Theo out of my mind.

"Or kill them," I said.

Chapter 9

Friday nights were not eventful for me. I wasn't about going to the mall to hang out with my friends or going to the movies when there was nothing but trash playing. Xandra was helping her mom in the ramen shop and couldn't hang out.

So I was stuck at home while Mom and Dad went out for a fancy date. I mean, good for them and everything, but oh so boring for me.

I hadn't been able to think of anything but Laura's vampire posse the entire day. Somehow, it was easier to look at the situation objectively. Maybe it was because it wasn't my life that was in danger.

Regardless, I wanted to figure out who these vampires were and learn everything I could about them.

It was like I was becoming a secret agent. Intel gathering, having stakeouts ... Ha, *stake* outs. I laughed at my genius.

I padded around the kitchen in fuzzy socks that were almost pointless in Florida, munching on leftovers. How does one go about acquiring intelligence on vampires? Well, you ask one.

I pulled out my phone, setting my chicken and rice casserole down, and opened the conversation to Iona.

So, I kinda got involved in helping that girl with her vampire problem.

Hit send.

I stood over my phone, shoveling spoonful after spoonful

of dinner into my mouth as I waited.

A few minutes passed, and no reply.

I groaned. Iona was predictable in this way, at least. Never around when I needed her.

I opened the message again and added another text. She was going to get them eventually, so why shouldn't I tell her what's going on while I wait?

I'm trying to figure out how to find these vampires on Instaphoto so I can get a little better idea of who we're dealing with. Any hints from a pro vamp to a rookie non-vamp?

I waited a few more minutes. No reply.

"Iona, come on. That was good. What are you doing, sleeping?"

I laughed again. She probably was.

I washed my dinner dishes, cleaned up the kitchen, and went to vacuum the living room and my bedroom like Mom had asked me to do. And came back, once again, to no reply.

Kinda feeling like you're ignoring me, I texted her. **I can see that you've viewed these texts. It's right there at the bottom of the message.**

Seen, 5:49 P.M. Come on, Iona.

My favorite cooking show was on, so I watched the chef make cinnamon rolls, a power food smoothie, and a death-by-chocolate cake, all the while my internal temperature rising to a gentle simmer as Iona continued to ignore me. When the show had finished—yep, you guessed it—still no message back from Iona.

I let my head fall back against the couch. "Ugh," I groaned.

Well, that was a dead end.

She was probably pissed that I'd decided to get involved against her advice. Which was fair enough, but I was surprised that she was choosing to ignore me instead of scold me or something.

She had been pretty clear since Byron had been killed that I needed to butt out of the vampire world. And I agreed with her, completely. But didn't she understand that I was the only one who could help this poor girl? Would she rather Laura get killed? Would she even care?

That made me angry.

Which then made me wonder why in the world I *did* care..

"Don't be an idiot," I muttered. "You aren't so heartless that you'd leave someone to suffer like you did."

I got to my feet and pulled my phone back out of my pocket. It was time to take matters into my own hands.

After giving them all of my personal information, including my date of birth, my favorite foods, what I had for breakfast, and the triglyceride level on my most recent blood test, Instaphoto finally let me create an account.

So long, privacy; hello, corporate spam. I guess it was a good thing that I signed up in my mom's name and with an email address I don't really use.

Sign-up process done, I had no idea what I was doing.

I started breezing through the How-To pages, which I barely read, and came to a "Suggested Followers" page, with a long list of names of celebrities, important business accounts, and some restaurants. Also, someone named Pauly Shore, whoever that was.

And I quickly realized my problem; I had literally no idea how to find the vampires, or their accounts. Searching for "vampire" definitely wasn't the way to it. I should know, because immediately after writing off that as a pointless idea, I tried it. No sign of Laura's stalkers anywhere—but there was plenty of vampire cosplay, themed parties, not to mention too many total weirdoes who thought they were *actual* vampires, drinking fake blood mocktails and showing off teeth filed down to points. The height of coolness, in their eyes; pure, distilled cringe to the rest of the world.

I drummed my fingers on the side of my phone, wondering what else I could look for.

An idea popped up, and I hesitated.

He wouldn't be that easy to find, would he?

I decided to try and typed in one word.

Draven.

And boom, there he was, right out there in the open for the world to see. I clicked on his profile picture, which was his pale face grinning at the camera, the skyline of Tampa stretched out behind him, reminding me of a king in his castle.

There were a lot of sinister pictures on his page. Most of them were of him at parties, with vampire women hanging off of his arms. Ballsy, being so blatant, but then there was nothing in any of his photos that screamed "undead." Someone who didn't know they were vampires would think that the red liquid in the glasses was wine.

I scrolled right past those pictures without looking too closely.

I stopped when a face in one of the photos was one I recognized.

"Well, well, well," I said.

The surly face of Mill stared up at the camera. He didn't look the least bit thrilled to be in the photo.

Bingo—he was tagged.

I clicked on his face.

Wait—*footballguy28*? Seriously?

Maybe "28" was the year he was born. Mill had posted only three pictures, the last of which was three years old. But that didn't matter; there was a DM feature.

Nervousness flared in me, but I hit the button to message him anyways.

Hey, we met at Draven's party a few weeks ago. Things got pretty intense and you had to help me to my limo. Remember me?

I went to browse through his three lonely pics when I saw he had messaged me back, almost instantly.

I remember. How are you?

Still breathing, thanks to you, I replied.

It was no trouble at all, really.

So formal, and so nice. Was it customary for vampires to make small talk? In person, he hadn't seemed like the kind of guy who talked very much in general. More of the grunting type. Matched his Cro-Magnon forehead.

That's good. So ... I had a question for you. Do you know anything about a bunch of vampires on Instaphoto? Like a gang of them? Causing trouble here in the Tampa area?

I watched the little ellipsis on the bottom of our

conversation as he replied.

It's not smart to talk over Instaphoto like this. A certain person whose party you crashed owns a large share of the company and may be able to monitor conversations.

My cheeks burned. Draven could be listening?

Oh, I was so not going to type his name into the search bar again.

Can we meet? Tonight?

The reply came back as I was still processing that last revelation. Vampire investors. I guess they had to pay for their pricey condos somehow.

I squinted at the reply. Surely I had read it wrong.

Nope. He was definitely asking if we could meet. Eager much?

But wasn't this exactly what I was hoping for? At least, in a way? I still needed help, and if talking over Instaphoto was going to be an issue ...

Sure. What were you thinking?

I didn't have to wait long.

The Half Caff. 8:00. See you then.

Chapter 10

The issue of how I would get a ride to the café was solved without much hassle. Xandra, who was finished at her mom's ramen shop for the night, texted me and asked me to hang out.

Perfect. I gave her the quick rundown of my current life situation. She was at my house in ten minutes, driving her dad's car.

The café was in North Tampa, the last shop inside of a strip mall. Not much to look at on the outside, but there was a nice water retention pond beside it. Even miles from the Bay, I could still smell the salt from the water.

"Never been here before," Xandra said, brushing hair from her face. A warm breeze swept through the night—spring had indeed arrived. Even the wussy Floridians couldn't complain about this.

A seagull cried overhead.

"It's odd to me that a ..." I caught myself. "That Mill suggested a place like this, don't you think?"

We stepped inside.

Cafés always smelled comforting to me. The intense, bitter coffee with the warm cinnamon and vanilla notes lifted my spirits.

"Oh, they have scones!" Xandra said excitedly, pointing to the bakery case beside the counter. Ample couches, wingback chairs and bistro tables were occupied with people. I scoured their faces.

"He's not here yet," I said.

Xandra's nose was nearly pressed against the glass display, the glossy pastries seemingly taunting her.

The rumble of a car engine nearly shook the windows. Almost everyone in the café turned to look.

In the brightness from the parking lot lights, a red 70s Mustang pulled into a parking spot right out in front of the café. It was gleaming, as if it had been polished that very day, with all the chrome finishes as clear as a mirror. The engine growled like a hungry tiger.

I may not know much about cars, but I knew that one was really cool.

And my mouth fell open as Mill stepped out of it.

He was dressed like a human, with a sleek leather jacket, blue jeans, and boots. And it *worked* on him. He might be dressed like the Fonz, but he sure didn't look like him.

The bell behind the door dinged as he stepped inside. He was so tall.

"He's *cute*," Xandra whispered. "You didn't tell me he was cute!"

"No ..." I mumbled in response.

I had to admit, he did look good. Really good.

But he's a vampire, he can't be cute! He's not even alive!

That doesn't mean he can't be kind of attractive, though. At least a little bit.

So went my inner dialogue.

He saw me standing there like an idiot in the middle of the café and started over to us.

No, he wasn't cute. That Cro-Magnon brow ruined his look. He was too surly.

Okay, maybe I can see it a little. Maybe.

"Hey," Mill said as he reached us. His voice was low, clear.

Somewhere deep down, I was pleased to hear it again.

"Hi," I said lamely.

He glanced at Xandra, who pressed herself up against my arm.

"This is my friend Xandra," I said, gesturing to her. "Xandra, this is Mill."

"Nice to meet you," Xandra said in the girliest voice I had

ever heard her use. She held out her hand, and he reluctantly took it.

I watched her eyes grow wide as her warm flesh touched his icy skin.

"Let's find a seat," I said, and turned toward the only corner that was unoccupied, out of earshot.

After we all slid into some barstools, I realized just how awkward this whole thing was. Why had I thought this was a good idea? I tried not to look at Mill, who was staring at me.

"So," Xandra said, drumming her fingers on the tabletop. "Vampires. Instaphoto. Who knew?"

Mill spared her a brief glance before he asked, "How did you find these people?"

"They found me, I guess," I said. I shrugged. "My neighbor, actually. She goes to my school. They seem to have a thing for her." I told him about the night before.

"Your neighbor?" Mill questioned, his dark brows wrinkling together. Where was the cute I saw a few minutes before? "How did you get involved?"

"My neighbor—"

"Your neighbor is not you. Why not stay out of it?" His gaze was hard, but it was easy to see he was concerned.

He was right. I mean, hadn't I been asking myself this same question for the last few days? I chewed on my lip as I formed an answer.

"Because ..." I started, and then sighed heavily. "Because it really sucks to have vampires rip apart your life and feel completely powerless to do anything about it. Or even be able to understand the problem."

"Oh, wow," Xandra said, putting a supportive hand on my shoulder. "I totally didn't even think about that." Hamming it up for Mill, I guessed, because that was *so* not a Xandra way of saying things.

Mill pursed his lips. Nevertheless: "Fair point," he admitted. "But still, you're up against four vampires. You really want to dive into those odds? Last time we crossed paths you were almost killed by *one*."

"Well, and Byron," I said, off-handedly.

He gave me a look saying that I was proving his point for

him but didn't exhibit much surprise about me being tangled up with Byron. Maybe he didn't know him. Seemed a stretch; I figured vampire society in Tampa was a small-town, tight-knit kind of thing.

"Right. Well, I could use some help, obviously," I said. It wasn't like he had to make me feel worse about it.

"These vampires … I think I know the ones you are describing." He stared at a scratch on the table's black surface. "They won't be easy. They're not young—"

"Big fakers," Xandra cut in, nodding her head matter-of-factly. "They dress young."

Mill raised a thick brow. "Appearances can be very deceiving with our kind." He leaned in. "They're old. Hundreds of years old. And what they're doing to your friend … it's not their first time. We fall into patterns, you see. And this one … in spite of the Instaphoto angle … has the ring of a very old, very well-trod pattern for this crew. They've done this many, many times before. Hundreds, probably. Maybe thousands. Of victims."

Xandra whistled through her teeth.

My throat tightened. I had promised myself that I was going to stay away from all of this stuff. I didn't think my psyche could handle a second round of all this crap.

Mill was right; I was in way over my head.

Chapter 11

If somebody had told me two days ago that tonight I'd be sitting in a coffee shop with Xandra and Mill talking about getting involved with vampires again, I would have slapped them silly. The aroma of coffee, which had smelled so good a few minutes ago, was now faintly nauseating. Xandra's pitying hand on my shoulder was making me twitch. And Mill's cool stare was enough to make my skin itch.

"Look," I said, snippily enough that Xandra withdrew her hand as if I'd stung her. "Byron overwhelmed me. These guys sound just as bad, maybe worse in their way. But ..." I looked pleadingly at Mill. "Somebody has to do something. This girl—she's kinda helpless, I'm sad to say. And ..." I swallowed my pride. "She's nice. She doesn't deserve this."

"'Deserve' rarely has anything to do with our fates," Mill said. "Did you know that Draven—"

"Is after me? Yeah." 'Deserve' damned sure didn't have much to do with *that*.

"Oof," said Xandra. "Biggest vamp in town, right? That Lord of Tampa or whatever?" She had found a coffee stirrer and was rolling it between her fingers.

"Yeah."

"Oof, times two," she said. "I'm starting to agree with your friend here. This is ... way out of our depth."

I looked at her. *Our?*

Mill began, "I'm sorry about your friend—"

"Neighbor," I corrected.

Mill's brow arched again. "People don't throw their lives all willy-nilly on the line for 'neighbors,' okay?"

Xandra gave a snort of laughter. "Points for use of the phrase 'willy-nilly' in this context." Definitely hamming it up for him. Ugh. Almost sickening.

"We're not friends," I explained, doing my best to shut out Xandra's fawning. "She's nice and all, but I don't know her that well. And my life's not on the line—yet. It's just ... starting to creep over it, or whatever."

Mill took a deep breath and exhaled slowly. Not for the first time, I wondered if vampires actually needed to breathe, or if Mill's sighs were just a habitual sort of thing.

"I haven't lived in a long time, I admit," he said slowly, "but ... even to me, this seems crazy."

"Oh, I feel you," said Xandra with an exaggerated waggle of the eyebrows. "It's crazy to us too."

I sighed, fighting against the aneurysm about to blow in my frontal lobe. "I know. But I just can't let her die—and that's where this is heading if I don't help."

Xandra's eyes widened, her reverie with Mill broken as the reality of the situation set in again. "You're right," she said faintly. "That's the logical end to all of this, isn't it?"

Mill nodded slowly. "It's how it always ends with our kind. Blood, life, death. It's a linear progression."

"So? Are you going to help me or not?" I asked.

Mill looked up into my face. His gaze was dark and contemplative. "If I don't ... you're not going to find them. So, in effect ... I'd be saving your life. But if I do that ..." He pursed his lips, shaking his head. "Am I doing you any favors? Treating you like a child, keeping you from making your own choices? I'd be like one of the Elder vampires, the ones who think you people are just herd animals, waiting to be culled at our leisure."

Xandra's face paled.

"That ... is a really disturbing insight into vampire culture that I'd hadn't fully considered. I think I'm going to go full vegan."

Mill bared his teeth in disgust. "Vegetables, ugh. Haven't you ever heard of a blood bank? It's a little more ethically sourced than most of your food."

Xandra was about to protest, but I stepped in. "Mill, are you going to help me, or do I need to stumble around outside Draven's penthouse looking for these people? Because I'll do it. I'm a kind of crazy that you vampires haven't seen before. I'm a teenager, okay? We don't just eat Tide pods to express our self-destructive natures."

The look that both Xandra and Mill were giving me were the exact same; wide-eyed, mouths slightly open. Clearly they preferred their detergent in their laundry, not in mouths.

But see, smartassery aside, I was totally lying. Because trying to help Laura was a *possible* death.

But stalking around outside Draven's penthouse? That was death guaranteed—the difference between trying to ride a rocket into outer space, and sitting underneath the launch pad when it lifted off.

"I'll help you," Mill said reluctantly. He reached into the pocket of his jacket and retrieved his cell phone.

He opened up the Instaphoto app.

"Man, everyone is on that site, even the undead," Xandra said bitterly. "My mom won't even let me play Facebook games."

I glanced at her. "Doesn't she know you've faced vampires? Feels like the internet would be a little less scary than Byron."

"I know, right? But I doubt she sees it that way."

Mill scrolled through a group of photos. "There's a hashtag they use to let us know when one of our own posts a photo. It's a subculture, subset—whatever you want to call it. Right here."

He pointed to the bottom of the photo's description.

"Ewww," Xandra murmured. "And also, that makes sense."

I stared at the hashtag. I probably never would have figured that out on my own, and yet it almost seemed too obvious. Hiding in plain sight ... or something.

"And they all use this?" I asked.

Mill nodded. "It helps the Elders keep tabs on us all."

I swallowed hard.

Two little words—two words to open up the entire vampire world before me.

#bloodknights.

Chapter 12

Was there anything more dramatic, overblown, and pretentious than calling yourself a #bloodknight? With your fancy hashtag allowing you to identify fellow *Blood Knights* as you all posted pictures of your fun, YOLO- (YOUO? You Only Undead Once?)-loving adventures all over the world?

I didn't think so.

I groaned as I closed my eyes against yet another vampire photo that made my stomach lurch, scrolling past it blindly. I was back in at home, in my room, doing research. Alone. Because Xandra had cooingly gone home to think about Mill or possibly sleep or something weaksauce like that.

But me? I was made of sterner stuff. I was sifting through the #bloodknights hashtag on Instaphoto.

Or maybe not. Because I hadn't made it through fifty of these pictures before I needed a break, afraid that my dinner might come back up all over the floor.

What a ridiculous predicament. These people—sorry, vampires—they were supposed to be humans' only predators. The unknown, unseen creatures that were the stuff of nightmares. Had been the object of *my* nightmares. Yet here they were, posting pictures of themselves about town with their fangs out, and showing off dark stains on their otherwise pristine clothing. They talked about the "sweet honey" they found down at the club or whatever. Which was disgusting.

But they didn't look any different than every other teenager in high school. They wore fashionable clothes, all of which were expensive. They went to coffee shops and posted cute, artsy pictures of coffee cups and books. And one of them even owned a cat and posted about it every hour on the hour. Should have hashtagged that one #catknights.

There was no overt violence, which I kept expecting as I scrolled. Violence was probably against Instaphoto's terms and conditions (gotta be honest—I didn't read them when I signed up), but even if not, I would bet anything that the vamp higher-ups prohibited it. No sense in drawing unwanted attention; their whole society would crumble in no time at all if they managed to get the attention of the human populace. However pedestrian the photos, however, they still implied the vampires' lifestyle, with red smudges on the fingers and faces of the subjects in the photos, all pale and all beaming— knowing that they could sweep under the radar so effectively, cold-blooded killers who were entirely unknown to ninety-nine point nine percent of the populace.

A quick knock on the door scared me so much that I threw my phone in the air. It hit the wall with a crack. I got off my bed to pick it up as Mom stepped through the door.

"You okay?" she asked, peering at me. She watched me stoop to pick up my phone from the corner.

"Yeah, fine; you just startled me."

Not to mention that she could have seen the weirdo vampire stuff on my phone. Too close.

"Oh?" she asked, leaning against the doorframe, crossing her arms over her chest. "What are you up to?" She arched an eyebrow. She thought I was hiding something, I'm sure.

She was right, of course.

I sank back down onto the bed, the scent of the lavender fabric softener in the sheets filling the air. "Not much," I replied. "Just thinking, I guess."

Mom's tight smile faltered slightly. Her brewing skepticism dissipated. "Everything all right?"

"Yeah, yeah," I answered. Typical teenager answer.

"I know you, Cassandra," Mom said flatly. "Something's bothering you."

"I'm just ..." I started. "I'm just tired."

She rolled her eyes. "Why do teenagers always say they are just 'tired' when they don't want to talk about stuff?"

The urge to just come clean about what was going on was strong.

It had been when Byron was around, too. I hadn't done it then—and look how things had turned out. How they *could have* turned out.

"It's just some stuff with Xandra," I said without thinking. "Boy stuff."

Mom visibly relaxed.

Guilt crept in.

Well, guess there went my short-lived non-lying streak. And I had been doing so well.

"So, how was your date with Dad?" I asked, trying to deflect her attention—and my own, from the sick twist in my gut. "Did you get something yummy?"

Mom's face split into a smile. "Ooh, yes. I got a perfectly cooked sirloin, with an herb butter that I'm determined to recreate. Dad got a delectable swordfish, so fresh and flaky. It was paired with these little potatoes that were unlike anything we've ever tasted."

"I'm glad," I replied. "That sounds good."

She yawned behind her hand, and then stretched her arms up over her head. "All right, kiddo. Dad's already in bed. I just wanted to check on you, make sure you were still alive in here."

"So far, so good," I said, and then laughed nervously, like an idiot.

She smirked, then turned to leave.

"Mom?" I said.

She turned.

"If you saw something bad about to happen to someone, and you thought you could stop it ... like a bus speeding toward them ... would you do it? Even if it meant you might get ... run over by the bus?" It sounded stupid even to my ears.

Mom studied my face for a second. I could tell from her eyes that her lawyer mind was searching for some deeper meaning. She shook her head. "It's not worth it," she replied, but there was a tightness in her voice. "You don't know that you'd be able to save them. It'd be better to just shout and stay safe on the sidewalk. You know what I mean?"

I understood, and normally, I'd totally agree.

"It's not worth throwing your life away." She took a deep breath and then snorted. "You should hear some of the cases I've dealt with in the past. Good Samaritan gets it in the neck for their efforts. Trust me, sweetheart. It's not worth it. Stay in your lane. Focus on school."

"But what if there was no other way?" I pressed. "If you don't do something ... something bad will happen?"

"That's awfully dramatic. Are you talking about Xandra here, honey?" Mom sighed, and then shook her head. "When you get older, you'll see. These sorts of problems won't be an issue anymore."

I nodded glumly, hoping she was right—fearing, knowing, that she was not.

"Don't worry, sweetheart. Xandra will be fine. Just be the good friend to her that I know you are."

"Yeah, Mom."

She gave me a final once-over, searching again for some sign about what I was keeping from her. Not finding it, she finally said, "All right, dear, I'll see you in the morning. Want to go out for breakfast?"

"The Egg-Cellent?"

She smiled. "My thoughts exactly." She started to pull the door closed. "Good night, sweetheart. I love you."

"Love you too, Mom."

And then she was gone.

Just be the good friend that I know you are.

Well, that settled it. I wasn't going to just stand idly by and watch from the sidelines—I would help, damn it. Ironic, considering Mom had been trying to talk me out of that very thing ... but what she didn't know couldn't kill her.

I mean, it hadn't with Byron, right? Uh ... nearly, but it didn't.

Stifling that thought, I reaffirmed my decision. No one else could help Laura.

Cops wouldn't get involved, and really couldn't; I'd figured that out pretty quick with Byron. And if Laura's parents were anything like my own, then they were totally in the dark, or wouldn't believe her. She might get thrown in the psych ward if she even opened her mouth. I mean, just look at her crumbling so readily when I talked to her about vampires. She'd kept her worries locked down, living in fear not just of the vampires, but of what people would say and think of her if she said the "V" word. And so, when I'd come along and spoken my truth, boom. She'd cracked easily, out of relief as much as anything else.

I knew exactly what that felt like.

Steeling myself,

I reopened Instaphoto, typed in the dumb hashtag again, and continued searching.

Mill said that this was the way to find them, and I was going to find them. The magic of social media. It had to be the only time I was grateful it existed.

A photo of a pale, blond male with his tongue pressed up against one of his fangs stared up at me, winking. He wore a green band tee and had styled his hair on par with a model. He was definitely one of the vamps harassing Laura the night before. Royal_Vee47 was his username.

I checked the date at the bottom of the picture. Recent—today. The location tagged him at *Zen*.

After a quick Google search, I groaned into my pillow.

Of course it had to be one of Tampa's most exclusive night clubs. Of course.

Chapter 13

To party with vampires, you will need the following:

#1: Clothes that fit their style. I started rifling through my closet, yanking and pulling anything out that looked remotely cool. (Note to self: in serious need of a shopping trip.) I decided on an ivory crop top that Xandra had loaned me, dark high-waisted jeans, and the same ankle boots I wore the last time I hung with the vamps. They had done me well then.

#2: You will also need jewelry, but nothing over the top. I donned a simple black choker, a few silver bangles, and a pair of diamond earrings from my dad. Just enough sparkle, yet not enough to draw too much attention. These vampires seemed to appreciate the finer things in life. Or afterlife. If I could show that I had some class or status, then maybe they would believe me to be one of them.

#3: I pocketed my cell phone. Vital if you're hanging out with vampires. I had Instaphoto ready to go, with notifications turned on for any new postings by Royal_Vee47.

And finally, if you are dumb enough as a human to spend any time with vampires, #4: you need a weapon. I opened my side table drawer and withdrew two thin stakes—another set I'd whittled (so I hadn't been completely relaxed over this past few months, okay?), reminiscent of that first chopstick-like affair from Iona. I put one in the waistband of my jeans, shifting it until I found a comfortable and secure position, and the other tucked in my messy bun.

It was sort of becoming my trademark look.

The old habit of sneaking out came back to me too quickly. Both Mom and Dad were asleep; their room at the end of the hall was dark, and Dad's snores were consistent. Content that I wouldn't be disturbed, I closed the door to my bedroom, threw open the window to the surprisingly warm night, caressed by the subtle saltwater mist blown in from the Bay, and slid out onto the roof.

It was too easy. I knew to slide my window until it was almost closed so I could sneak back in later. I knew where to step so I didn't slip or make noise. And I knew the best place to lower myself down off the roof and fall lightly to the ground below. Down here, where the fence blocked the soft, sea-borne waft of salt, the night smelled of grass and sulfur; the neighbor's sprinklers were on. Their chittering, popping spray was my soundtrack.

I quickly made my way around the yard and down the sidewalk. My Uber was waiting, idling at the sidewalk. I hopped into the back and told the driver where to go.

Quiet, still suburbia flashed past as we drove.

I spent most of the ride fighting with myself. I wanted to look composed when I pulled up. I had to own it. I had done it once, so I could easily pull off the vampire thing again, right?

Right??

Next question was, what was I going to do once I found these vampires? Talk to them? Ask them about their latest conquest in some sort of bizarre paranormal small talk?

No, maybe not even that. This would only be a quick visit—just recon. In and out, and then I was going to leave. Easy, right?

I was insane.

The club was in an inconspicuous brick building in an old part of town. Normally, I would have gone right by the place, thinking it was some old factory or something. Several stories tall, the windows were blacked out, and the fire escape looked dangerously unstable.

Once out of the car, I could hear the dull rhythmic thud of bass.

A crowd of people, or maybe vampires, were gathered in front of the only door. Everyone was easily two or three years older than I was, some even more. They were all dressed for the club; short skirts and low-cut tops, tight jeans and bright colors.

I stepped up to the crowd and fell into the line leading to the door. A couple of glances were all I was spared before people returned to their barely paused conversations. Good—I wanted to stay very much on the down-low here, at least as much as was possible. Carefully, I studied those nearest me. Even up close like this, I couldn't tell who was a vamp and who was a regular human. Maybe, if I was lucky, the only vampires here would be the ones I came to see.

Taking my phone out, I double-checked the vamp's profile. He'd added another photo, just five minutes ago. Now the ringleader girl vampire was here, too, hanging on his arm.

Another tag for *Zen*. They were inside. And suddenly I didn't want to be here.

But I had reached the front of the line. I looked up at the bouncer who didn't even look at me as he waved me inside. No questions, no ID check, nothing—which was good, because in my haste to act, I hadn't exactly considered how I'd get in, seeing as I was underage. Probably my pass was my chest—which should either be met by a burst of righteous indignation or relief that I'd been allowed in so easily. Or both. But with vampires perhaps all around me, that issue was the least of my concerns right now. I walked through a long hallway, bathed in blue light. The music had doubled in volume, a throbbing bass thudding through my bones. Every pulse of it flooded my veins with a deep sense of fear, danger—and just a little thrill of exhilaration, sickening and morbid and addictive all at once.

I followed the hall to a narrow staircase leading up. At the top, there was a glass door.

The music hit me like a tidal wave as I pushed it open. Blinded by neon lights in every color, I stepped through.

Chapter 14

If the first vampire party I attended was all goth and glamour, this one was all punk and pandemonium. The air was hot and thick, like an early August afternoon, but nowhere near as pleasant. Silhouettes of bodies pressed together filled the room.

The room itself wasn't all that big but was seemingly endless in the dark. The bar at the opposite end of the room was lit with a tube of blue neon snaking around the top of it, and tables were scattered along the wall on either side, with people standing, sipping brightly colored or glowing drinks.

Not for the first time, I wondered if I had found my calling as I stalked about the room like a secret agent. Who knows; maybe there was some sort of secret government supernatural task force. Maybe I could get hired just based on experience.

I stayed close to the outer wall in the shadows, and as I drew closer to the bar area, I saw the ghostly pale skin and silvery blond hair that belonged to vamp I had seen on Instaphoto. It was long on top, styled like a wave in the surf. When he turned his head, it held its shape perfectly.

I rolled my eyes. He had more product in his hair than I did at prom last year in New York.

He was standing with a few other vamps, all of whom looked as if they stepped out of a teen style magazine.

The girl had perfect hair, flawless makeup, and stilettos that could double as a weapon. Roxy, was it?

Another male there was as gorgeous as Byron had been; long, flowing locks, laidback demeanor, an attractive smile.

The last one looked like he was Italian, with dark hair and features. He was built like a linebacker with rippling muscles and a strong jaw.

They wore wry smiles, and danger flashed in their eyes.

I froze, suddenly realizing that I had literally no idea what I was going to say to them. I mean, was I insane?

Oof. How many times in the past few months had I asked that question?

Scanning the room again, I found the sign for the restroom. I needed a minute, just a minute, to figure out what the heck I was going to say to these creatures.

I pushed the door open and was grateful when I found the sleek, modern restroom empty. I slipped into a stall and locked the door behind me, leaning back against it.

"You are an absolute idiot, Howell. A real class act."

Well, at the very least the vamps weren't bothering Laura right now. The longer I could keep them here, maybe find out a little bit about them, the longer she was safe.

I pulled my phone from my pocket and opened a message to Laura, whose number I had because she had given it to me months ago when she'd done her whole welcoming me to the school gig. No, I'd never called it before, or texted her, because ... well, at the time, I kinda thought after she'd peeled off from her intro that there was no way she could have been sincere when she said, "Hey, if you ever need anything, or just want to talk, call me, text me, whatever?"

That was Laura.

Hey, I need you to listen to me, okay? I sent. **Stay in your house tonight. Don't go out anywhere. And especially don't let anyone inside. I'll be in touch.**

Who was I, Iona? That text sounded way too much like her.

With Laura out of the firing line right now, I at least wanted to figure out what this motley crew wanted with her.

Unfortunately for me, that probably meant a conversation, since eavesdropping wasn't going to cut it—people didn't just spill things like, "Hey, that girl we're vampire stalking?

Let's talk about our motives and plans for her!" casually, in public, for people like me to hear.

Mind made up (and stomach unhappy with the decision), I stepped out of the stall and up to the long mirror stretched over the marble sinks.

It was time to bring Elizabeth back out of hiding.

"You did this once, and Draven believed you," I told my reflection. "You can totally fool these eternal *Teen Cosmo*-reading losers. You are Elizabeth, a vampire, and you have every right to be hanging out at a super cool place like this and just happen to run into some other vampires."

I brushed a curl from my forehead back up into my bun.

"Own it, girl," I whispered, and then made my way back out of the bathroom. I sounded confident, but like everything else that had brought me to this point in my life … it was a big, fat lie.

The music was even louder than I remembered it, pushing in on my ear drums like I was twelve feet underwater. I spotted the vamps again, grateful that they hadn't made their exit while I was in the bathroom. I pasted on a cocksure smirk and kept it there as I walked across the dark room to the bar area, and the table where they all stood. The scent of alcohol clung to it like a cloud, its edges diffuse, mixing with the musky cocktail of too much cologne—or just too much Axe, which made me concerned for the number of men who hadn't realized it wasn't a crowd-pleaser when they were fourteen.

"Can you believe him?" the blond male was saying derisively. "It's not like he's my dad or anything."

"It's really all the rules that suck," the silvery-haired girl said, shaking her head, her waist-length curls swirling. "He just can't let us have any fun, can he?"

"Total buzz kill," the dark-skinned linebacker replied. "He's just a tyrant."

The long-haired male laughed. "Wouldn't it be nice to just hit him where it hurts?"

"Yeah, but how?"

That was my cue. I stepped up to the table—to the surprise of all the vamps there.

All of their eyes on me almost made me lose my cool, but I leaned on the table between them all.

"You want to get Draven mad at you?"

I looked at each of them in turn. It was obvious I was an unexpected, maybe unwelcome visitor to the party. But I definitely had their attention. And that meant that I had the control in the situation.

Be bold, be confident. Most importantly, be cool. The vampires will listen.

Their gazes were dark, considering.

I allowed myself a low, short chuckle.

"Just do what I did—go to one of his parties ..." I paused for extra effect. It worked. Their eyes were fixed on me. "... And kill one of his loyal subjects."

Chapter 15

Take a breath, Cassie. That went as well as a line from a movie.

My words hit this group of forever-teens like a bomb. The girl, Roxy, stared at me through slit eyes, her jaw working. Her blood red fingernail rapped against the tabletop.

Her trio of male hangers-on watched me cautiously. The handsome one almost seemed amused, a smile tugging at the corner of his mouth. The linebacker's eyebrows were up near his hairline.

The blond, however, scoffed at me, an eyebrow arched, skepticism etched on his features.

But I held my ground. How could I top what I just said, really? So I just watched and waited, overconfident smirk plastered on my lips, my gaze firmly on theirs.

I was owning it. I had to keep owning it.

Finally, after an excruciatingly long moment, or century, I wasn't sure, the long-haired Lothario type at the opposite side of the table grinned, showing his fangs.

"I heard about that," he said appreciatively.

Now I understood. The silence wasn't really because they knew I was a human girl walking into a club like a lamb to slaughter. No.

They were *impressed*.

Well, all except the girl with hair like moonlight who had now crossed her arms and pursed her lips.

But that didn't matter. I had them, had their attention.

The males all moved closer together, making room for me at the table.

"That was you?" the swarthy vamp asked. His accent bore a faintly Italian lilt.

My smile widened. The best lies you don't even have to speak.

Wait. I actually did kill someone at Draven's party. Whatever. The lie was that I was a vampire, blending in with vampires.

"That's the first time I've ever heard of something like that happening right under Draven's nose," the blond male said, running his fingers through his styled hair. "Everybody was talking about it."

"I heard he was uber pissed," the linebacker added. "Theo was like a nephew to him or something."

"What is this, *The Godfather*?" I said before I could stop myself.

To my great surprise and relief, they laughed. Even the girl smirked a little, her eyes never leaving my face, some of her ice beginning, very slightly, to thaw.

"So, what did it feel like?" the Italian one asked.

"What, you never killed a vamp?" I asked. I nearly choked on my tongue. Definitely should have said "another vamp."

They all exchanged glances, shaking their heads.

"It's not exactly an easy thing to do," the blond male said.

"And it's kind of taboo," the linebacker added. His eyes were big, but he was clearly trying to pretend that he was cool enough to handle taboo stuff. A real push-the-limits guy here.

Ha. Taboo among vampires. Wait until I told Xandra.

I cleared my throat. Another human thing, I reprimanded myself. But I grinned. "I got him alone. He didn't even know it was coming, Draven's little pet," I said, my voice as smooth as velvet, almost purring.

But my stomach was churning as the images flashed across my memory from that night—the images that had filled my nightmares for months: Theo launching at me, his arm wrapping about me as he pinned me to him, grip so powerful it was near unbreakable ... the sight of his fangs, mere inches

71

from embedding in my neck, draining me ... and the panicked, flailing way I'd fought back, managing by luck more than anything else to push the stake through his heart. Even the way he had seemed to dissolve into a tar-like pool of black goo had haunted me, the stale, rancid, bloody smell of it—

"He thought that he would be a gentleman," I said, "helping out a girl like me, new to town. He made it too easy, really. I played coy, timid, the little mouse. I could tell that he thought he was some big–city hot shot. Made all these grand statements, trying to impress me."

I dropped my voice.

"I saw right through him. He started asking questions that he had no business asking—" the male vampires' eyes grew wide. Apparently, privacy was important to them "—and when he asked me to step outside with him, I knew what he was—a direct pipeline to Draven. A perfect chance to strike the Lord right in the teeth."

They all flinched. Mental note: apparently vamps took their teeth seriously. Maybe there were vampire dentists dedicated to this cause.

"What did Draven do to you?" the blond vamp asked hesitantly.

"You really want to know?" I replied. I think I was enjoying this a little too much. "He killed my lover of seventy-two years." Low hisses. Their awed looks softened.

"So this was super personal?" the Italian one asked gently.

"You have no idea," I replied. "An eye for an eye, that sort of thing.

"So, here we are, out on the balcony with all of Tampa stretched out below us. Theo was careless. He let his guard down. He turns to me, all smooth and handsome, trying to put a move—

"And then," I said, considering taking the stake out of my hair but deciding against it, wanting to keep that as my secret weapon secret a little longer, "I stabbed him through the heart with a broken chair leg."

Always good to sprinkle some truth in ... even if that was Byron who caught the chair leg, not Theo.

"Whoa," the linebacker murmured.

"Tough luck for him. Wrong place, wrong time, you know." I waved my hand dismissively. "I stepped back inside, had a few drinks, laughed with some friends, and then ran into Draven before I left. Of course, he thought I was trying to sneak away without him seeing."

I smiled. "He did exactly what I expected him to. You hear the stories about his ego. That he likes to project the image that nothing happens without his say so, that he notices everything in his territory." Or so Iona had suggested, at least as related to vampire activity. "I kept up the coy new-girl act." I grinned. "And then I looked Draven in the eye and we laughed like old friends before I walked right out the front door … after killing one of his dear ones under his nose."

There was dead silence as I wrapped up my story. Seconds passed where their faces were all unchanged; baffled and in awe.

And then, all at once, they all started cheering and slapping the table and laughing heartily.

"Wonderful!"

"Stunning!"

"Five stars!"

They clapped for me. *Clapped.*

"Well done," the Italian one said, his impressed smile still on his face. "You are one brassy dame … what's your name?"

"Elizabeth," I replied automatically. It came so naturally, it was as if it had been my real name all my life instead of just my middle name, forgotten except when I was filling out paperwork that required it. Where the male vamps praised me, though, I noticed now—Roxy hadn't shifted much at all. She was unreadable, impossible for me to penetrate … yet as I turned my gaze to meet hers, the frostiness emanating from her was tangible.

Guess that little smile earlier hadn't been the first signs of her thawing after all.

I had seen her acting in Laura's backyard. She was the alpha. That was why she was studying me as closely as she was. I could tell in the way that the males glanced at her, in the way they carried themselves around her. She was the queen, and these were her worker bees.

The males, I had won over. But Roxy ... she wasn't going to allow a competitor into the pack this easily.

"Hey, Elizabeth, you should come with us," the linebacker said, elbowing me in the arm.

"Yeah, you should!" the blond one said.

Roxy rolled her eyes.

"We were just about to ... go do something more fun."

Oh crap. That was probably vampire talk for probably go kill someone. Especially since they hated Draven, who was all about keeping things on the down low.

I hoped that the color disappearing from my face went unnoticed.

"Oh, yeah?" I said. "Where are you going?"

Roxy was the one who replied, with a flick of curls over her shoulder. "You'll see. Come on."

And they just left their empty glasses and walked away from the table, through the writhing crowd of bodies.

The blond male stopped just outside the crowd, his face bathed in red light.

"Come on, Elizabeth."

I followed, of course, because ... this was the point. But ...

I had a feeling this wasn't going to end well.

Chapter 16

It turned out that we were heading to a limo. And it was no ordinary limo, no.

It was leather-lined, LED-lit, and hand detailed. Real wood inlays and crystal glasses and a dark green bottle full of something I had no desire to know anything about. Compared to this, the limo Iona had sent for me looked like a thirty-year-old pickup truck. Under other circumstances, I could get really excited about taking a ride in this thing.

Not when I was taking a cruise with a bunch of hell-raising bloodsuckers, though.

Nestled in the backseat, feeling like the centermost in a tin of sardines though I had plenty of room, I finally learned all of their names. Roxy, the Queen Bee, I knew, but pretended not to. The gorgeous one with the long hair was Charlie, and the linebacker was Ivan. The blond male, who seemed to be the second-in-command, was named Benjy.

To the tune of music so loud it threatened to burst my very human eardrums, they really let loose in the limo. Since there weren't any humans around, they didn't have to hide their true selves. So their laughter was louder, their movements swifter, and their actions rougher—almost like the way they'd unleashed chaos in Laura and Gregory's backyards. It frightened me, but my entire life literally depended on acting like it was no big deal, like I expected nothing less from them. And so I threw myself into it too, using the hysterical edge that was rising in me to force the laughter. Roxy stared, fixated at me. Her eyes watched my every move. I flashbacked to Theo, and how I hadn't taken that situation seriously enough. If I said or did anything weird or out of place, Roxy would sink her fangs into my neck without a second thought.

The boys seemed entirely at ease, though, like a bunch of frat guys: punching each other in the arms, teasing.

"So you guys are never going to guess what happened the other day," said Charlie, slinging an arm around Benjy's shoulders.

Benjy leaned away from him, trying to duck out from under his arm.

Ivan leaned back in his seat, crossing his arms over his chest. "Oh?"

Charlie sneered. "I was late for a meeting with George—"

"Typical," Benjy chided.

"I came across this guy who was walking home all alone. I remember thinking that it was just too easy, you know? Humans have gotten so much more cautious at night. I hardly ever see one out in the open."

Roxy arched an eyebrow.

Charlie glanced at her briefly, and then went on. "I was a bit thirsty—"

Oh, please stop right there. If I throw up partially digested leftovers all over your fancy limo, you aren't going to be very happy. Also I'd be discovered, and I really can't deal with that right now.

"I figured Draven couldn't be all that mad at me if I didn't actually kill him. So I called out to him, and you know what he did?"

I winced and was glad that Roxy's attention was on him for the moment, and not on me.

"He ran."

Ivan's amusement disappeared. "Did you go after him?"

Charlie shrugged again. "Nah, man. It wasn't worth it, you know?" He chuckled low in his throat. "Besides, I don't think I could have caught him all that easily in the state I was in."

Benjy groaned and his head fell back against the seat. "Don't tell me you were using again?"

"We've talked about that, Charlie," Roxy said coldly.

Charlie looked at her, and I saw what looked like fear pass over his face. But his face smoothed again, and he laughed. "Well, it was probably better that way. I wouldn't have been much use to George if I was hungover, you know?"

So even vampires used drugs of some sort? And did he mean hungover like ... from feeding?

I wished I was wearing a long-sleeved shirt that would have hidden the goosebumps that had appeared on my arms. Glancing out the window, the dark streets of Tampa sped by, a series of streetlights and cars all passing in caramel-tinged streaks from the tinted windows.

No one had told me where we were going. I could've maybe asked—it was a perfectly reasonable question, vampire or not—but the time had long passed. With my fear of detection—Roxy had eyes like my mom's, far too assessing—and the fact I was *very* outnumbered, I couldn't afford to draw any more attention than necessary.

So I got a ride full of stressful wonder, just to spoil this limo experience even more.

I didn't think we were heading to Draven's place; these guys wouldn't be very excited to go there, even to keep up appearances.

But were we going to Laura's?

What would I do if we did?

At least I had forewarned her. If that's where we ended up, I would fill her in about it later. And maybe I could convince them that she really wasn't worth their time.

But we turned off the highway onto another road along the Bay, slowing to merge with traffic. Maybe I could make an excuse, get myself out of here—another Uber. If they were going to find some humans somewhere to drink deeply of, I wanted zero part of it. It would totally give me away—but I'd reveal myself when I passed out from the sight of the blood. Better a natural escape than shoot myself in the foot after all this work, right?

I was just about to open my mouth when I realized that the limo had come to a stop. The boys all scrambled to get out, talking animatedly again.

Roxy glared at me before slipping out gracefully.

I was glad I didn't bash my head climbing out.

And my mouth fell open. We were at the Tampa International Airport.

"Wait, where are we going?" I asked, turning around to them.

Ivan grinned, and pointed east, his European accent coming through.

"Miami."

He was joking, right?

… Right?

Chapter 17

Of course they had a private jet. They were beautiful, jet-setting vamps, and the night was young. Why wouldn't they have a private jet? I guess when you're immortal, you can accrue a limitless amount of wealth, and buy things like limos and planes.

Perched on the toilet with my head in my hands, I was trying not to pass out from panic in the plane's bathroom, which, though small, was also sleek, metallic, modern—think the highest-end bathroom in a showroom, but compacted a little.

Did that trick with breathing into a paper bag actually work? I was willing to try pretty much anything. And the sharp stench of cleaning solution in here was making me dizzy.

What to do? In moments, the plane would lift off, trapping me on it, thousands of feet in the air in the middle of the night, with four vampires who could drink me dry. If they didn't, in short order I'd find myself in freaking *Miami*.

Perhaps worst of all: my mom was going to kill me if she found out I was gone. I pulled out my phone and opened up a text to Xandra.

I may have made a mistake. I tracked down those vamps chasing Laura, and long story short, I'm on a plane with them heading to Miami.

I sent it to her, and then copied the message to Mill, Iona, and Gregory. I wanted someone to know what happened to me if I was dead before we landed.

I added a second message to Xandra: **Can you cover for me somehow with my mom if it comes to it? I'll owe you again. Big time. I'll get you that anime set you've been eyeing.** Hoping for the best, I switched my phone onto airplane mode. Not a light decision—this was my one lifeline over the next few hours, or days, or however long we were in Miami. But I didn't want any texts coming in and freaking me out. They wouldn't help me now, anyways.

I knew that the vampires were going to wonder what in the world I was doing for so long in there, so I snapped a few selfies. That's what girls did in the bathroom, right? And I'd have proof for them if they asked.

I took a deep breath, trying to steel myself before I unlocked the door.

And there was Roxy, right outside, all perfect curls and rose-and-lavender perfume.

Her hand was on her hip, head tilted to the side. Her eyes flashed dangerously.

"Why were you in the bathroom?" she asked tartly.

I held up my phone, the pics I had taken still glowing on the screen. It wasn't my best selfie ever, but with puckered lips I figured I was selling it. The peace sign with my fingers wasn't a bad addition either. So *kawaii*, as Xandra would say.

Ivan and Benjy appeared in the narrow doorway.

"There you are," Benjy said, beaming.

Roxy shot him a nasty look over her shoulder, and he recoiled as if she had hit him.

"It's a private plane. I had to take a bathroom selfie on it. It's practically like an FAA requirement," I giggled and shrugged my shoulders. "Couldn't resist."

I tossed a big smile at Benjy, who returned it, though less enthusiastically than before.

"Guilty of doing the same thing," Benjy said. "I have probably taken a thousand pics in the bathroom. Makes us more *human*, amirite?" He snickered.

Ivan nodded. "It's a new plane. I snapped a few outside myself."

He flashed his phone, the picture already posted on

Instaphoto.

Ignoring Roxy's hard looks, I followed the boys back to the seats at the front of the plane.

"We should get a pic all together," Benjy said. "Commemorate the moment."

I froze, my knees turning to jelly. I suddenly realized that Draven would find me a lot faster if any of these vamps put my face on their Instaphoto page.

Thankfully, the answer came quickly. It helped that I had to have this conversation with a friend back in New York so my Mom wouldn't catch me at a party.

"Look, I'd really appreciate it if you guys didn't tag me in your photos," I said in a voice as nonchalant as possible.

They all turned their attention to me, Benjy with his phone's camera already on.

The engines outside rumbled to life, and my fear levels spiked. I hoped that my acting skills could hold out for the plane ride.

"Draven, you know," I went on. "I had to deactivate my Instaphoto account now that he's looking high and low for me. Kill one little minion at his party and he suddenly he wants you dead," I said dryly.

Charlie and Benjy chortled.

I pulled open my phone and scrolled through some photos. Not a whole lot of selfies—that wasn't really my scene—but I flashed a few to the boys, to approving nods, and lied, "I'm chipmunking some good ones for after all of this blows over."

"Total bummer," Charlie remarked.

"Yeah, that totally sucks," Benjy said. "But don't worry. We won't tag you in any pics. It'll be our little secret." And he winked at me.

"Thanks," I said. Then I added, steady and cool as possible, "I'm sure Draven won't be a problem for me much longer."

A bold thing to say, I realized too late. My statement seemed to suck all the air out the cabin. Eyebrows raised. The amused smirks on the men's faces faltered, replaced with disbelief. I'd been avoiding Roxy's laser gaze lest it burst open some kind of truth valve and made me spill all my secrets, but out of the corner of my eye, I could see her expression tighten.

These vampires had to know I was a threat though, even if right now we were all buddy-buddy. The reminder of Theo's murder had garnered me laughs. Draven, though, was a whole different kettle of fish—and, I should've known even as I was saying it, way ridiculous. Threatening to off the Lord of the entire Tampa territory? That was stupid-ballsy.

Ivan's face darkened. He glanced at Roxy.

Yeah, I definitely went too far there.

The moment passed, thankfully, and the others became absorbed once again in their own phones. Roxy in particular threw herself quite furiously into texting, taking advantage of the last few minutes of service before takeoff.

What made it all worse was how on top of all of this, I hated planes. My knuckles turned white as I gripped the arm of the seat.

"Hey, Elizabeth?" Charlie asked, putting his phone down on the table in front of him. "You okay?" He snickered. "You look a little pale."

I smirked, but my stomach churned angrily.

"I just …" I started, avoiding looking out the window. "I hate flying."

"You too?" Ivan asked. He shook his head. "I get it. I hate heights too."

"It's not heights," I said, swallowing hard. "It's the—" And then I realized that I had no idea what would be believable for a vampire to be afraid of. It's not like they would necessarily die. I really hated the turbulence, the complete lack of control if the plane were to just tumble out of the sky. But a vampire wouldn't care about that.

"It's the time it takes, isn't it?" Benjy asked, inadvertently throwing me a bone.

I grasped it with a hard nod.

"Definitely. It feels like such a waste of time."

"Well, I guess that you haven't learned that time really is meaningless to us, have you?" Roxy retorted. "How old did you say you were?"

"Seventeen," I answered automatically.

Roxy smiled, but it didn't reach her eyes.

"Right, and I'm twenty," Ivan replied, winking. He stood and crossed to the mini bar along the wall. "Who wants some bubbly?"

The boys all heartily accepted.

Roxy, though, shook her head. So did I. I didn't want to know if this "bubbly" was champagne or ... something else. With the boys distracted, I muttered to Roxy, not bothering to hide the annoyance in my voice, "I'm ninety-seven."

Roxy tossed her hair. "Like I thought. You're just a kid."

She really had no idea how right she was.

Chapter 18

I don't think I had ever been quite so excited to feel a plane start to descend. It was almost three in the morning, and I was starting to have some serious déjà vu from my last set of late-night run-ins with vampires.

Miami, I reflected, looking out the window, was much brighter from the sky than Tampa. A bigger, older city, it stretched out along the coastline like ink spilled across paper. I had never been to Miami before; I'd only ever seen it in movies and in photos.

The vamps were just as excited as ever. They had apparently moved past my awkwardness, because we had spent a good fifteen or so minutes trying to take the perfect selfie with the right lighting in the dark plane, with them promising time and time again that they wouldn't post any photos with me in them. It was all very nudge-nudge, wink-wink—like I was some sort of celebrity. In a way, I supposed I was, to them anyway—the killer who dared defy Draven right under his nose and got away with it. And they were the privileged few to know the truth about my identity.

For such inhuman creatures, it was a strangely human way of behaving.

Not for the first time tonight—not even for the first time this year—I wondered how they'd failed to detect me. It was the same at Draven's party: I strolled right under their noses, a prey animal whose heartbeats they could surely hear. Yet these vamps seemed to take my lies at face value. Because of my skill?

Or was it something darker—that lies were distinctly human, almost depraved—and these monsters were ... shudder ... better than that?

It was an unsettling question, and not one I could have answered without coming clean about my un-undeadness.

Another limo was waiting for us as we stepped off the plane.

Benjy seemed to think it was amusing how much I didn't like planes, laughing it up at my relieved expression when we finally touched down. I played it off as boredom as best as I could.

"There's still a fear of death in the best of us," Charlie whispered to me as we waited for Roxy to slide inside the limousine. "I still hate going on boats. And I was a sailor when I was alive."

That sort of made me sad.

Then I remembered their harassment of Laura—the reason I was here in the first place—and my sympathy flew out the window.

The limo here was just as decadent as the limo in Tampa. Who was paying for all of this? I slid my phone out, thumbing airplane mode off. It buzzed softly as texts came through, the opening lines of each cycling in a banner across the top of my screen. I squinted, desperate to open them—

"Selfie?" Ivan suggested.

"Oh, yeah," I said, swiping the notifications clear and opening the camera. "Let's do it."

They all crowded into the narrow frame of view, and we snapped away like crazy, playing with filters and contrast levels. With each shot, I hoped that they didn't see just how paper-thin my pasted-on smile was—and that they didn't detect the quick beating of my heart in anticipation of reading my texts. Shame it was damned near impossible for the moment.

"So," Roxy said coyly, her eyes flashing. "Elizabeth. Where are you from?"

"New York," I replied. "But not the city. I'm from a small town closer to Syracuse. You wouldn't know it."

Roxy crossed her legs and narrowed her eyes. "So you know Lord Kirkwood?"

I had two choices here. The look on Roxy's face made me seriously consider the answer, and I knew that too much time thinking would be a giveaway as well.

I couldn't help but feel like a mouse deciding whether or not to take the cheese on the mouse trap.

"Who?" I finally decided to ask.

"I've never heard of him either," Benjy replied. "I thought Orfeo was the Lord of New York?"

Unbelievably grateful to Benjy and his unknowing support, I nodded at him. Being a liar, I could recognize the truth when I heard it. "Him, I know."

Roxy was like a smoldering coal; all I would have to do to set her ablaze was poke her and prod her a few times.

What I needed was a huge bucket of water.

The thing I was starting to appreciate about Roxy was that she wore her emotions on her face as clear as day. Most dramatic women did just that, and I was glad to see that the snide and snarky tendencies of teenage girls were the same across the living and undead.

It was almost a breath of fresh air being able to discern what she was thinking about me. Byron had been a nightmare in part because he was so unreadable.

I knew that Roxy hated me. Why, I wasn't exactly sure, though I had my suspicions vis-à-vis her alpha status in this group. It had to be that; if she suspected I was a human, she would have ended me by now.

Did she think I was lying about killing Theo? Ironic if so— that was pretty much the only thing I had told them all night that was true.

The boys had opened the sunroof, and Benjy and Charlie had stuck their heads out. We could hear the muffled sounds of them shouting out into the Miami night, the bright neon lights of the shops and clubs and restaurants all along the side of the street casting dizzying snakes of muted color into the limo.

Ivan was snapping selfies.

Roxy's scrutiny of me once again passed; she returned to

her cell phone, tapping away with pursed lips.

I took the opportunity to check my texts.

The replies were all from Xandra and Gregory, and exactly what I expected: complete and utter freak-outs. I replied, letting them both know I was in Miami, and that I would keep them posted. I wished I could have explained more, but at least they all knew I was alive.

Nothing from Mill (no surprise), and nothing from Iona.

Something about Iona's lack of reply made me a little sad. I guess now that Byron was out of the picture, our business was more or less concluded.

Still ... with Xandra and Gregory, it was nice to tell more than one person that I was alive and know that they actually cared.

The vampire boys were YOLO-ing their way through the night, laughing and hooting, like regular teenagers out with their friends—or vampires harassing a human they intended to turn, I thought grimly, as their behavior tonight was not much different to when they'd been in Laura's backyard.

Roxy's moodiness apparently didn't faze or dampen their enthusiasm. She was sitting back against her seat, twirling a gold ring around her middle finger, with a look on her face that said someone had peed in her O-neg-flavored Kool-Aid.

The limo made a sharp left turn and slowed to a stop. The boys ducked back inside the limo, talking over one another about the club we'd pulled up at, the lights, the people.

Another club? I knew that these guys weren't living anymore, but wasn't this exhausting to them? I was young, and I was tired just thinking of all the crap we'd done tonight. Netflix was waiting at home, and *Pretty Little Liars*, and I longed to watch other people spin lies instead of doing so myself at great personal risk.

This place looked a lot more like a club than the last place—a glass and steel building, with silhouettes in every window.

Benjy clapped me on the shoulder before climbing out of the limo.

The shrieks that greeted us were terrifying. I thought someone was dying, but instead, it was a group of people standing near the doors behind a rope fence.

"It's Roxy! Did you see her?!"

"Roxy, oh my gosh, will you sign my bag?"

"Is that Benjy? He's so hot!"

Huh. Vampire Instaphoto fangirls. Well, I never. Charlie's arm was around my waist, grinning at the crowd. Benjy snapped another selfie us as we stood in front of the crowd. I smiled like the fool I was as they guided me past the throng and into the dark.

Vampire internet celebrities. Great.

Chapter 19

The inside of the club was what I would expect the inside of a castle to look like—stone walls, low-hanging chandeliers, torches on the wall. Miami's lights could be seen through the many tall windows surrounding the space, but inside, it was medieval, dark, and moody. I half expected people in black capes with high collars to jump out and scare me from around the archways surrounding the room.

My nose wrinkled as we stepped fully inside. There was a sharp, metallic tang to the air, like rusted iron.

The dance floor itself was sunken into the middle of the room, and the floor was made from scorched wood. The music was more my speed than the last club, with more techno, and less rap. The pulsing lights were absent, but people were packed in here like more tightly. Except these weren't people. These were vampires—all of them.

Well, almost all of them—I saw, with an icy lurch of horror, in one corner of the room, men and women barely older than me, arm in arm with vampires—who held leashes that drooped from their hands and affixed to collars at the humans' necks.

Stomach heaving, I watched as one of the vampires nuzzled his face into the crook of one the girl's necks, almost as if to kiss her, and sunk his teeth into the tender flesh.

A dazed look passed over the girl's face, and she slumped into the vampire's arms.

I looked away before I fainted. Just across from me, on a

curving seat, one poor girl who couldn't be any older than seventeen was—I hoped—passed out. Her handler loomed over her, leash in hand, dark splotches on his crisp white button-up.

Did these vampires have no shame? Of course they didn't. This is what vampires did. And I was fully aware of it. If media depictions hadn't prepared me, hearing it first-hand from the vampires I'd met should have done.

I ... just had never seen it before in person. Up until this point, it had all been theoretical.

I wished it could have stayed that way.

The injustice of it just curdled my blood. These humans were being used as toys and pets—like dogs, but less. I knew that Draven and his underlings felt this was all humans were good for—he'd called us *cattle*—but everything in me just wanted to rescue them. Fortunately, the fact that I was so ... perturbed, disgusted, horrified ... went unnoticed, both by my temporary group of "friends" and the vampires in the club who had no eyes for me, but did shoot my new "friends" admiring looks and waves. So I meandered along behind, keeping a tight lid on my expression—lying with my face—as best I could, as we clambered stairs to a glass-encased room along one wall.

The room was a little quieter than the rest of the club, the glass blocking out some of the thundering music. A few round tables, also glass, were scattered around, and all but one were entirely full. Roxy and the boys walked over to it as if it had beckoned them. I followed quickly after.

The entire club was visible from this room, even the gross feeding corner. I tried to sit with my back to it, but it didn't make the reality of it any easier to deal with. I was sure that image was burned onto my brain.

Great. More nightmare fuel.

What in the world was I doing here with these vampires? How did I get myself in this deep? All I wanted to do was figure out who they were and what they wanted with Laura. So far, I had learned nothing.

The only way that I was going to be able to stop them from harassing Laura for sure was to kill them.

Could I even do that again? Could I take out four of them, clearly working as a pack, when I'd barely managed to luck my way through two one-on-one encounters before now?

Iona was right. I really should have stayed out of all of this.

Problem was, I couldn't make an easy escape now. So I had no choice but to go deeper—yet the deeper I got, the harder it would be to dig my way out. And the worse it was going to be if they found out that I was a human. Which meant that I *had* to kill them.

They chattered—conversations that were so *normal*—totally unaware that, as I sat beside them, I was frantically plotting their demise. Benjy had started on about trouble with his cell phone, and Ivan was listening intently. Roxy was reapplying her lipstick in a small compact mirror.

She glanced up and caught me staring at her. Her face hardened before I looked away as casually as I could.

Charlie tapped his foot to the beat of the music. He smiled at me.

"I'm going to go get a drink," he said, rising gracefully to his feet.

"I'll come with you," I said. "I need to stretch my legs." I stepped away from the table with him.

Sitting at that table any longer might have driven me insane. The less time I had to be that close to them—Roxy in particular—the better.

"You doing okay?" Charlie asked, hands in his pockets.

"Totally," I said. "It's been nice to get out." Was he seeing through me right now? How much of my worry, my fear, was I showing?

Charlie smirked. "Nothing better than being able to hang out with our own kind, you know?"

I unconsciously looked over into the feeding corner. The girl who had been bitten before was standing again. It gave me very little relief. "You aren't kidding."

"You want a drink?" he asked, gesturing over to the bar in the corner.

Why was there a bar when there were humans all over the room? I gritted my teeth behind my smile as I shoved those thoughts from my mind.

"I'm good, thanks," I replied, trying not to sound disgusted. "I'll catch up with you in a bit."

Charlie shrugged and turned toward the bar.

I exhaled a breath I wasn't aware I was holding. I turned and looked around the room.

Somehow it was harder to look at all of the vampires around the room when I was alone. I knew I looked like an idiot just standing there, so I pulled out my cell phone out and spun on the spot, the vast group of vampires behind me. Masking my photos as club selfies for Instaphoto, I banked them for Xandra later. She'd go nuts when she saw them.

If she saw them.

Caught in the front-facing camera as I twirled, Roxy and Benjy and Ivan sat together at their table inside the glass room. All of their eyes were on me. Roxy pointed at me. She was tight-lipped and glaring. Ivan seemed pensive; Benjy was frowning.

My smile faltered, but I fought to keep it in place. They couldn't know I'd noticed. Nevertheless, I made sure to snap a photo with all three in the background. It might prove useful to show Iona or Mill later on. If Roxy was going to keep her eye on me, I was going to do the same to her. Turning again, I pretended to check my hair and makeup in the camera.

What was I going to do? How in the world was I going to get out of this? Was it possible that I could just hop back on the plane with them back to Tampa? Could I just outright ask them about Laura?

I was pretty sure my whirling thoughts were about to drive me absolutely insane when I heard a piercing scream. The atmosphere shifted instantly. The dancing stopped. All the joy of the vampires and their pets was replaced with confusion—and then, hardly a moment later, shrieking panic as a column of fire lanced up near the bar. Something was aflame, burning with a noxious smell, and the screams mingled as vampires backpedaled, moving away—

I gasped, eyes widening as the throng near the bar parted to reveal—

It wasn't some*thing* burning.

92

It was some*one*. And as they thrashed, gripping their face, shouting wildly, I saw—

Long hair.

It was Charlie.

A loud, blaring alarm rang through the air, inciting more screams and pandemonium. Then the sprinkler system kicked on, turning the room into a wet, misty mess.

It was too late. Charlie's skin was melting off in dark, thick globs. Screams dying in his throat, he collapsed against the bar and rebounded, falling into a still heap. Flames eating at his skin, he was already decaying into black goo, spreading across the floor like the limbs of a starfish. A hand snatched me around by the arm. I yelped, wheeling around, wide-eyed—

Benjy.

"Elizabeth, are you all right?"

I nodded, easing my arm out of his grip even though I desperately wanted to yank it free. "Yeah," I said. Water stuck to my eyelashes and dripped off the end of my nose. Suddenly I was cold.

Benjy looked over at the bar. His eyes were wide with grief and shock. Vampires and their pet humans continued to shove past us, embroiled in a terrified panic that threatened to turn the club into a riot.

"Come on!"

Benjy and I turned. Roxy was standing just off the dance floor. I could tell she was doing everything she could to not look over at the bar.

We didn't waste any time. We joined the throng flooding the doorway back outside.

The sound of a fire truck in the distance greeted us as we stepped out into the humid night. Vampires were running down the sidewalks in both directions. I could still hear the fire alarm blaring inside. What were the firefighters going to think when they found what was left of Charlie's body? Not to mention all of the blood around …

None of that mattered. What was important was that Charlie was dead—and I hadn't needed to lift a finger.

One down. Three more to go.

Chapter 20

Ivan was standing off to the side, already waiting. He saw us and waved us over. His face was blank. Benjy pulled out his phone and stepped aside, one hand to his ear to block out all of the noise. I heard him say the word "limo."

Roxy was livid. Her eyes blazed as she paced along the sidewalk.

"Did you see that?" Fear riddled her voice. I was surprised, honestly—she'd barely broken her icy façade during my time in her company, and I was beginning to suspect that nothing would crack her.

On the flipside, the fact she was asking meant that she wasn't suspicious about my part in Charlie's death.

"It's kinda hard to miss a guy spontaneously combusting at the bar," I said.

Benjy rejoined us. "Limo will be here in a minute," he said in a low voice.

All of the energy that had been present from the moment I'd met this group was gone, replaced with a fraught unease.

Benjy had a distant stare. "Can you believe that?" he asked, sounding choked. "Someone slipped Charlie holy water."

So that was what happened. I'd never have guessed, not least because the one time I'd used holy water against Byron, he hadn't caught fire. I guessed this was the difference between a light splash and actually ingesting it.

Thing was—who had slipped him the holy water? And why? Based on the faces of the other vampires, I wasn't the only one wondering that very thing.

Benjy was wringing out the corner of his shirt as the limo pulled up. Roxy waited for Ivan to open the door and then slid inside. I hurried to stand beside Benjy. Ivan barely glanced at me as I joined them in the limo. The fear of them leaving me behind was evidently unfounded.

The limo pulled away from the curb as soon as Roxy slammed the door shut.

It felt strangely empty without Charlie's calm, cool presence inside the car. And out of all of the vampires in the group, he was the one I hated the least. Which was a weird thing to think, after seeing him terrorize Laura with the rest of them, but this was getting to be an increasingly weird life.

Roxy was like a simmering volcano. Her face, darkly pensive, was almost a snarl.

Ivan was leaning forward, the tips of his fingers pressed together, his eyes on the floor.

Benjy was rambling.

"Can you believe that?" he said again. "Who would have done that? Who would even dare?"

I would have, I thought. I definitely would have. It was a great idea. I planned to keep that in my back pocket. Maybe Mill had a secret supplier and would be willing to share them with me.

Roxy turned her gaze on me. Suspicion clouded her eyes.

"Did you see Charlie talk to anyone? You were closer than we were."

Ah. Yes. About that. I definitely was closer than they were. But she was watching me the entire time I was away. Really, she hadn't stopped looking at me since I joined their little posse earlier that night. But it wasn't like I could say that out loud.

Roxy's gaze hardened. "You left with him. I saw you talking to him before he walked over to the bar. What did he say to you?"

I racked my brain, realizing belatedly that whatever he had said to me were pretty much the last words he ever said.

"He didn't say anything important," I replied, shaking my head. "He asked if I wanted a drink. And asked if I was doing all right."

Roxy clicked her tongue in disgust.

I shot her a nasty look of my own. "And he said something about how it was nice to be hanging out with his own kind."

Benjy's lip trembled. "I just can't believe ..."

"Did he say anything else?" Roxy snapped.

"No," I said. "Nothing."

Her expression was tight, disbelieving.

A thought occurred, and I pulled my phone out of my pocket. "I was taking selfies when it happened. Let me see if maybe I caught something in the background."

I scrolled through my selfies, making a point to avoid the ones with Roxy, Benjy and Ivan in the background.

"Let me see," Roxy said, sliding over to sit beside me.

The last three photos I'd snapped were of the dance floor. The first one of those captured a good portion of the room. The bar was in the background—blurry, but I could make out Charlie standing with his back to my camera.

Roxy snatched my phone out of my hand. "Who is this?" she snapped.

"Who?" I asked. She'd grabbed my phone away and was holding it up to her face, pale skin aglow with digital light.

She zoomed in on the photo and then turned the phone, showing it to me. Someone was standing beside. Someone male. Someone tall. Someone ... handome. Ish.

Someone I recognized. Fighting to keep my composure, I stared down—at Mill, a drink in his hand ... offering it to Charlie.

Chapter 21

Roxy was actually snarling. Her hands were knotted in her long curls, and her fangs were bared. "Who is that?"

Benjy pulled my phone out of Roxy's hand and looked at the photo before passing it to Ivan. He didn't seem as convinced as Roxy was.

"I don't recognize him," Ivan remarked before handing my phone back to me.

"Probably because he's from the Miami territory," Benjy said.

"Why would some random Miami vampire have killed Charlie?" Roxy spat. If her temperature grew much hotter, she'd catch fire from her own anger—two in a night, an excellent result for me, if a little hazardous right now as I sat beside her. "It doesn't make any sense."

"Maybe he just likes to kill for fun? Gets his kicks from it?" Benjy asked.

Ivan crossed his arms. "It is unlikely, but I have heard of some vampires who have so lost their humanity that they can only feel alive by doing something as extreme as killing another vamp."

"Charlie is dead," Roxy said. "Someone murdered him." She gritted her teeth. "I don't believe for a *second* that this was an accident. Someone had it out for Charlie. Or for us."

"But who do we know in Miami?" Ivan asked. "Roxy, this is crazy. I'm upset about Charlie's death, too. But … murder? Why?"

Benjy put a gentle hand on Roxy's arm. She shoved him off. "Ivan's right," Benjy said, trying to conceal his hurt feelings at her rejection. "I know you're upset. But we don't know what happened, really. We don't even recognize the guy that did it. Assuming he really is handing him holy water."

"You think he's handing him a vodka chaser?" Roxy spit, acidly.

"I've seen this guy before," I said quietly, staring at my phone in concentration. Another lie. Well, this was the truth, but understated. A lie of omission.

All three heads spun in my direction.

"What?" Roxy asked, a slight hiss manifesting in her speech.

My brain had been spinning through their entire conversation. I knew eventually they'd place Mill. They might even be able to track him back to Draven's party, and the two of us walking out together post-Theo. That was a nice little mine that could blow me up at any time, detonating all my lies in one spectacular BOOM that would end in three very angry vampires descending on me. Long odds, but not ones I wanted to play at the moment.

Besides, why keep it bottled up when I could spin a lie into it and use it to my advantage? Voila, suddenly "Elizabeth" has useful information. We'd better keep her around! Besides, if I did it right, I could steer these vamps in a completely wrong direction.

Roxy smoldered. "How do you know him?"

I drummed my fingers on the leather seat, still staring in concentration. "He was at Draven's party."

"Who was he there with?" Ivan asked.

"Theo," I said. Sticking to truth could only work in my favor. Other vamps could back up my story. "I met him— briefly—before Theo tried to get me alone."

"What was he like?" Benjy asked. He was leaning forward in his seat.

I shrugged my shoulders. I had to tread very carefully. I wanted to divert their attention from Mill, who was going to get an earful when I spoke to him next. He may have been protecting me by offing one of them, but surely he must have realized that by doing what he did, the remaining three would go to high alert, seeking revenge?

"He hardly said a word to me." I finally pried my eyes off the picture on my phone. That part was true. He hadn't really spoken to me at all until after Theo was dead and he found me on the balcony, clutching my stake, washing Theo's blood from my hands in the pool.

Benjy frowned. "Theo was one of Draven's favorite underlings. Always did what he was told."

"That's what you think," Ivan replied. "Theo had a habit of sneaking off and having his exploits plastered all over the newspaper the next morning in the form of a missing person."

"So this guy, Theo's friend. Did you get his name?" Benjy asked.

"I did, but I can't remember it." Eyes looking up was the signal that you were trying to recall something.

"Think." Roxy was cool, a little snap to her voice.

"Something with an M ... Mark? Michael? Melbourne?"

Roxy opened her mouth to lash out, but Ivan stepped in.

"Rox, if she doesn't know, she doesn't know. Give the girl a break. She had other things on her mind during that party."

Roxy glared cool daggers at me from across the limo.

Benjy looked at Roxy, rubbing his hands along his pants, leaving dark smudges. I guess vampires did sweat. "You think this guy knows we're plotting against Draven?"

I didn't know which was better; for them to think that Mill actually had been Theo's friend, or that he was happy to see him dead. My head was starting to spin trying to figure out the web of alliances in Draven's territory.

"Maybe he was getting revenge for his friend," Roxy said, turning her hostile gaze on me, as if she had read my thoughts.

Now that I had owned the fact, I needed to stand up for it.

"You think that drink was meant for me?" I asked, trying to seem just a touch rattled. You know, as one would be following a failed assassination attempt. I couldn't help throwing a dark spin on it. "I mean, normally I'd be mad if someone stole my drink, but in this case ..."

Roxy did not find that amusing.

"If this guy was there for me on Draven's behalf," I said slowly, "I'd be a pile of black goo right now. Draven's not subtle. Holy water? Not his style." I shook my head. "No, something else is going on."

This was all true. Well, except for the black goo thing, and maybe the timing of wanting me dead. But there definitely was something else going on. If these guys knew I was playing them, there wouldn't be an ounce of blood left me in.

"If this guy was watching me," I went on, "then they would know that we literally just met tonight. Why would Draven strike one of your people? Why not just ... kill me?"

Roxy hesitated. Good. I found a weak point. I pressed on.

"Killing Charlie to hurt me makes no sense, because it wouldn't ... hurt me. It didn't."

All three of them glared at me, their eyes blazing.

"Not that I'm not sad and freaked out about his death," I added, holding my hands up defensively. I really had to stop talking before I thought about what I meant to say. "What I'm saying is that Draven is a lot more cunning than that. He was making a statement here. Not to me—he'd do that by ripping my entrails out and exposing me to daylight. I think this one ... was to all of you."

Benjy, Roxy, and Ivan all exchanged uneasy looks. The fact that even Roxy showed a flicker of doubt ...

Man. I was suddenly so very glad I worked my lying game to A++ before getting cast out of New York. If I'd stumbled into this as some sweet innocent—like Laura—there was no way I would get out alive.

Scratch that. Survival still wasn't exactly guaranteed.

"You know ... I think she's right," Ivan finally said.

I wished I could have sighed with relief. I'd successfully pushed the attention away from Mill and me, and back onto Draven.

I should be working for the CIA or something. I had gotten so good at lying that I had just convinced a bunch of vampires that the vampire I knew that had killed their friend to protect me hadn't actually been behind it.

I was even a little surprised myself.

"Why would Draven kill Charlie?" Roxy asked.

Ivan's jaw clenched. "It is very hard to believe that Draven would punish us this harshly just for complaining about how he runs things."

"You don't think it's because of Charlie's ... activities, do you?" Benjy said. "Draven really doesn't like leaving a trail of bodies. Not in his territory."

"I told Charlie to clean up his act." Roxy grimaced. "I didn't think it'd get him killed, though."

It was odd to me, sitting there with these vamps who were as good as enemies to me. We all had the same enemy in Draven, though. It was like some weird hate triangle.

"I need to know who's behind this. And if it is Draven, then he's going to pay for what he did. Nobody crosses us, not even the Lord of the territory," Roxy said.

Benjy and Ivan both looked apprehensive, a fine return to when I'd talked about removing Draven earlier. Silence fell, and I didn't dare break it.

Roxy blazed like a phoenix in the throes of death. "We've been attacked ..." she said, slowly, pronouncing every word clearly in the interior of the limo, "... this means war."

Chapter 22

We arrived at the airport a few minutes later. Roxy's face was set in a steely, determined expression. Ivan and Benjy were giving her a wide berth. I happily followed suit. Clambering back aboard the plane, my heart constricted when I saw the empty glass that Charlie had been drinking out of, exactly where he had set it down before disembarking.

Stop it, I cajoled myself. *He harassed Laura with the rest of them. He deserves no pity.*

I took my seat beside Benjy and was glad that no one felt the need to fill the silence with small talk. If they wanted to grieve Charlie, then I was more than happy to give them the space to do that. It meant that I didn't have to fill the time with more lies. Which was getting exhausting, even for me.

I pulled my cell phone out, let everyone—including Iona—know I was on my way back to Tampa, that I was fine but had a lot to tell them.

Mill received a very different message from me.

What in the actual heck were you thinking? Thx for the backup, but the Instaphoto gang saw you in one of my pics. Told them I recognized you from the party but didn't know you. Hope you had a good reason for what you did. On our way back to Tampa now. Meet soon?

I hit send, deleted the message, and then turned my phone on to airplane mode.

The tension in the cabin was palpable. Roxy had her arms wrapped around herself, and she was chewing on her bottom lip as she glowered out the window.

Ivan was scrolling through pics, and I saw him hesitate—snaps with Charlie.

Benjy was lying with his head back against the seat, staring up at the ceiling. Unlike the flight out here, this was subdued. The frenetic energy was gone. Little was said between us. The noise of the engines pervaded, rather than the laughter of three friends joshing each other like college-aged boys on a night out. Which was what this was, I supposed—what it had been.

Periodically, throughout the flight, Roxy would let out a low, primal sort of growl. It made me flinch every time, but she was too busy looking out into the twinkling, starlit darkness.

Twenty minutes after we had crested above the clouds, however, she shattered the silence with another pronouncement.

"We need numbers." She was gnawing one on of her fingernails. She turned her beady stare on Benjy. "We're turning that girl tonight."

My stomach plummeted.

She was talking about Laura. She had to be. I guess it was possible that they were harassing some other poor girl, but they had made it pretty clear that night in her backyard that they wanted her to join their posse.

I was trying to keep my face blank, but it was really tough when my telltale heart was thundering against my ribs.

Grimly, I realized that I'd made matters for Laura a whole lot worse. In getting involved, and drawing Mill out here to intervene, I'd caused this little hole to open in Roxy's clique. Laura was in grave *and* immediate danger—and it was my fault.

Worse: right now, I had no way of telling her what was coming. And odds were that I wouldn't have a chance to talk to her until it might be too late.

My future came down to two choices. I could let these vamps follow through with this decision, or I could stop them.

And stopping them meant killing them.

Two stakes. Three vamps.

This was going to be interesting.

The plane descended through clouds intertwined with silvery moonlight. The near-silence between us had lifted now, or at least was trying to: Benjy kept trying to engage Ivan in a conversation, but Ivan wasn't interested. Between attempts, he kept throwing nervous glances toward Roxy, who was still glaring out the window. She was all puffed up like a bomb ready to blow. Familiar, salty air assailed me as we clambered off the plane. I'd been an off-and-on fan of it since moving here—off because it reminded me that I wasn't in New York anymore; on because there was something strangely addictive about the tang blown in from the Bay— but this night it meant I was home, so I was most definitely leaning toward the "on" side of things. The time on my phone was just before three in the morning. Dawn was still a few hours away, but I needed to make my getaway fairly soon; I couldn't exactly fake sizzling in the sunlight.

"Get the limo," Roxy said, pointing at Benjy. "I want this done before the sun comes up."

Damn—Laura had three hours. Tops.

I was going to have to deal with this sooner than I was ready to.

Ivan followed Benjy out of the hangar, and Roxy turned on the spot and stalked off toward the office. Probably to pay the fee for the charter.

Was it possible that they had willingly separated? And that her back was turned to me? Checking for the stake in my hair—still there, unnoticed—and the one in my waistband,

I waited until Roxy's heels had clacked her out of sight, then slipped behind a red cargo container.

I gently pulled the stake from my hair, and my curls tumbled down over my shoulders.

I literally had one chance to do this. She wouldn't linger in the office long. I had to make my move if I was going to.

I tried to move, but my feet wouldn't budge.

When I'd killed Theo, it was a sudden and defensive sort of decision. It wasn't premeditated. Not like this.

What I was planning ... if you left out the fact they had already died ...

Was murder.

But Roxy wasn't human. I couldn't get thrown in jail for killing someone who wasn't alive anymore. She wouldn't leave a body behind for the police to discover. She would just cease to exist, becoming a room temperature slick of black goo.

But what if … what if I didn't make it? What if it didn't work for me? What if the third time was a charm—but for bad luck?

I'd thought about my death a lot over the last few months. I was only seventeen. It didn't seem fair for someone as young as I was to die. Because even if they decided to turn me as punishment, I'd still be dead. I wouldn't be able to go home to my parents, or stay in Tampa.

What was it about me that made me jump into harm's way so easily? Was this bravery? Lunacy? Maybe a little of both?

My hand tightened on the wooden stake. I wished I had sanded it down a little more; a few stray splinters poked the tender skin of my palm like miniature wooden vampire teeth.

Roxy was standing in the doorway of the office. I could see the man behind the desk who she was waiting to speak with; he was on the phone, chatting to someone on the other end like it wasn't three in the morning.

I took a few deep, quick breaths before pushing myself away from the cargo containers and across the room toward Roxy, as silently as I could. A breeze blew, hard. Sea air was overridden by the scent of diesel. It came in a great gust, the smell, like a tanker had spilled beyond the doors of the hangar.

The man behind the desk rose to his feet, pointed at the phone to his ear, and mouthed to Roxy—apologizing for needing to take the call. A very important matter, apparently, albeit a very *funny* matter, going by another hearty laugh that rattled him as he turned and stepped farther into the room. A heavy door on the other side of the building squeaked open, and then the man's voice disappeared as the door slammed shut. Roxy didn't turn. She crossed her arms.

It wasn't difficult to imagine her tight-lipped expression at being held up.

What on earth was I doing? It was like my body was on autopilot, and my brain was yelling hysterically for it to stop.

Have you ever watched a horror movie when the character starts to hear their heartbeat in their ears? And they start to get tunnel vision? Like time itself has slowed down. I felt like it wasn't me, it couldn't have been me—

My mouth was dry. All I could taste was the gasoline in the air. My fingers gripping the stake were freezing and as white as bone. The hairs on the back of my neck stood up straight.

I was five feet from her. Four. Less than three.

How had she not heard me yet? Did she care? Did she even suspect me?

I sucked in a sharp breath through my teeth as I pulled my hand back to strike, and then struck Roxy square in the back.

Clink.

The stake collided with something hard—and, like armor, utterly impenetrable.

Roxy whirled around—but I only caught a glimpse of her fiery stare before hands wrapped around my waist, wrenching me away from her.

I was thrown through the air, tumbling over like a barrel down a hill. I yelped—then slammed the floor, all sense of up and down momentarily lost. Benjy stood over me, fangs bared.

"What do you think you're doing, Elizabeth?"

I edged backward—

He moved so fast I didn't see it. One moment he loomed; the next his full weight was pressed against me, a hand wrapped around the stake still, somehow, in my hand.

I shrieked, jerking out a flailing kick that he ducked too easily—then rolled, stake under me as I slipped out from beneath Benjy. He just chuckled—like Byron.

Which was a disadvantage for him. It pushed the fear aside and coaxed my anger to the surface.

He lunged at me again, weight pressing down against my right arm—

I didn't even wait to see. I thrust out with the stake in my left hand, and felt it sink into flesh.

At the same second, a searing pain flared up my right arm.

Benjy screeched, relinquishing his grip on me. I scrabbled away, free, widening the span of hangar floor between us—

Stake buried in his chest, Benjy writhed. Mad, wild eyes, all whites, stared above him as he hissed, clutching at the wood sunk into his heart, body contorting like something out of *The Exorcist*.

It was too late for him. His skin was already dissolving, decades of long-postponed decay finally setting in. Black blood ran from the corners of his mouth, out of his ears. A sulfurous stench came with it, nauseating and powerful.

Far-off, I knew that I should feel a surge of victory. But this was so sickening, so horrifying to watch again—so I scrabbled away.

Pain shot through my forearm again—a long, bloody scratch, running from my elbow all the way to my wrist.

I touched it with trembling fingers.

"Well, well, well," said Roxy, over the last wheezing breaths left Benjy's body.

She stepped past it—what was left of it, anyway. Her eyes were wide with surprise, but more sickeningly, with delight.

"What do we have here?"

I stepped backward, brain still running at half capacity, knowing only that I couldn't penetrate whatever armor she wore, so I should run, now—and clanged against the red container. Roxy knelt down in front of me, and ran a thin, white finger down the length of my arm, as if to use my blood as paint.

"Our new friend is still living after all." She smiled, but it quickly turned to feral disgust. "At least ... for another few seconds."

Chapter 23

I ran. Or, I tried to. My feet slipped out from underneath me as I fumbled to stand, and I fell back onto my knees.

Roxy grabbed the back of my shirt, snarling—but I pulled free, escaping only because that first accidental stumble had been enough for her to drop her guard, to underestimate me.

I surged out of the hangar, feet pounding on concrete.

This couldn't have gone any worse. There was absolutely no way that could have been worse.

Well, Benjy could have killed me. That would have been worse. I guess.

But if I'd been killed, then at least I wouldn't be terrified, running for my life.

The grey light of the moon peeked through the clouds overhead. No time to admire its beauty now though. Besides, stark lights along the runway threatened to overpower it. A pure, glowing white, they were near-blinding as I sprinted past, over places where water had pooled from an overnight rain, puddles reflecting dazzling white pockets of light.

Roxy howled behind me. Her heels sounded like bullets against the tarmac as she ran. She was going to catch me. A cry of pain up ahead drew my attention to—

"*Mill?*"

He was locked in a brutal UFC-style fight with Ivan. Black, tar-like blood was spattered everywhere. One of Mill's arms was coated in it. Half of Ivan's face was too.

Both vampires were grimacing from their wounds and

moving incredibly quickly. Every hit resounded, far too loud to be without consequence.

My heart skipped. My mind seesawed—between fear that Mill would lose this fight, and hope—

Because he was my only chance at getting out of here alive.

"Mill!" I shouted, waving my hands wildly, like a tourist greeting an old friend at the airport. Or any idiot. Both, really. He turned—

Ivan surged across the space between them. Fingers curled into claws, he sunk them deep into the flesh above Mill's navel—and tore open a new, oozing wound.

"Mill!" I screamed.

Mill staggered back, grabbing at the hole in his gut, blood like pitch spilling out between his fingers.

He couldn't die. He couldn't. If he died, then that meant …

I didn't stop running. I tried to read Ivan and Mill, knowing there was very little, if anything, I could do if I reached him. If Mill was able to get me out of here, then maybe we could still escape. But I wasn't sure how badly hurt he was.

My breath was coming in rasps, and I had stitches in my side. I couldn't keep it up. I couldn't—

I hit the ground. Hard. My chin scraped against the pavement, and I felt most of the skin on my palms rip to shreds. Pain exploded from my ribs—broken?—somehow setting off ringing in my ears like a grenade had gone off beside me. I tasted blood.

In my dazed state, it took me a few seconds to realize that I hadn't tripped. Roxy had slammed into my back, bowling me over like a tenpin. She leered down at me, straddling my chest.

"You think that you're so smart, don't you?" Roxy asked, brutally cold edge in her voice. "You thought you were so clever, playing vampire the way you did. And to think—you almost got away with it."

She pinned my arms up over my head—and then dug a thumb into the scratch that was Benjy's parting gift.

I shrieked as white-hot pain lanced through me. Tears stung the backs of my eyes.

"Please—"

Roxy pulled her long curls over her one shoulder and bent close to my face.

"I knew something was wrong with you. Something … off." She let a whiff of blood out like a breath. "I should have guessed when you locked yourself in the bathroom." She bent even closer and whispered right in my ear. "I have a sudden opening in my squad, Elizabeth. I need some viciousness on my side, and girl—you fit the bill. Your looks aren't quite what I expect, but right now? Beggars can't be choosers. You can make me look better by comparison. Get ready to take selfies with me for the rest of your existence." She grinned, fangs extended.

I slammed my eyes shut, whimpering, fighting to escape—but she was too strong, I could barely buck beneath her.

She leaned forward—I felt her crossing the last of the distance between us, her icy skin a hair's breadth from mine—

Water rained down, as though the heavens had opened and the earlier rain had resumed.

Roxy screamed. Recoiling from me in an instant, she leapt away from me as though I'd done it. Hands clutching her face, she screeched, a banshee's wail that tore through the night.

Holy water.

And there was Mill, glowering darkly over Roxy.

In one easy motion, he lifted her and threw her across the tarmac. Then, without a second glance at her, he slipped his arms underneath mine and lifted me. Then he was running.

Over Mill's shoulder, I saw Ivan run to Roxy who was lying on the ground, still clutching her face, howling like a rabid animal. Ivan was holding his own face, and he was leaving slick, dark streaks behind him.

I was going to be sick.

I laid my head against Mill's chest. Everything ached, every small bump in our hectic escape sending stabbing pains into my chest and arm. When Mill finally slowed, I looked out from his chest to see we'd made it to the parking lot. He had stopped beside a black limo, just like the one that Iona had sent for me months before.

I recoiled. Limos were going on my hate list. I wanted nothing to do it with it.

Mill gingerly put me on my feet.

His shirt was bloody—with my blood—and I was drenched in his, the black, tarry substance caked all over my side.

If he hadn't pulled open the door, I would have vomited right there. Somewhere in a deep recess of my mind, I wondered how Mill wasn't going absolutely insane with my blood all over the place. Blood. Vampire. How?

I clambered in, tears welling up in my eyes again. I'd definitely cracked a few ribs. And it was way more painful than I had ever thought it could be.

Mill slid in beside me as if he didn't have a hole in his stomach as big as a fist.

He slammed the door, and then pounded on the window to the front. It slid down, and the man at the driver's seat did not seem remotely surprised to see us there.

"Floor it!" Mill ordered.

The man did not hesitate. He threw the car into drive, and we peeled out of the parking lot—leaving Roxy and Ivan behind us.

Chapter 24

The limo squealed tires out onto the highway, and I felt better with every car that pulled up beside us and in front of us, camouflaging us amongst the traffic. Not that you really *could* camouflage a stretch limo amongst regular traffic, but still. With Roxy and Ivan dealt with for now, I was acutely aware that I was sitting with another vampire and covered in my own blood—and his.

Frantic, I ripped a corner of my shirt off, and tried to press it to the wound in his stomach.

"Don't worry," Mill said gently, placing his hand on my arm. "I'm fine. Really."

I stared at him, dumbfounded. He had literally just saved my life. And not for the first time.

"What are you doing here? And how are you not dead right now?" I asked. "You're bleeding … everywhere …"

Mill winced, hand hovering over his stomach. "I'll be fine. Vampires heal pretty fast. And I didn't die because my head's still intact, and he didn't use a stake. Make sense?"

"You can't just lose too much blood?"

He shook his head. "It doesn't really work like that with us. We heal a lot faster than we can lose blood. Now, if he had kept at it, he could have incapacitated me enough to kill me. That was his plan." His face darkened. "And mine, as well."

I grimaced.

"I'll be fine by tomorrow," Mill went on. "This won't kill me."

Silence fell for a few moments as we weaved in and out of traffic.

"Mill ..." I said. "Why did you come all the way to Miami?"

"Following you," Mill replied. "Trying to help."

I rolled my eyes, laughing hollowly, and wanted to cry at the same time. He had no idea how much those words meant to me, and yet ... everything turned upside down when he showed up.

"You texted me, remember?" Mill said, the black flow of blood slowing as it rolled down his shirt and pants.

"Yes," I replied reluctantly, but I frowned at him. "I didn't intend for you to *follow* me. Mill, you almost got me killed!"

I sounded like an ungrateful brat. He had just *saved my life*, and all I could do was accuse him of interfering? It wasn't like I had it all under control in the first place.

Mill's brow furrowed.

"I was trying to help. You were on a trip with four vampires."

"Only two now," I pointed out. Which I should've been happy about—but having stoked the fires of Roxy's wrath, no longer able to fly under her radar, and seeing the sheer damage Ivan had done to Mill, I wasn't feeling super optimistic about that right this minute. "Roxy thought I had something to do with Charlie's death. She said as much to me once we left the club in Miami ..."

Mill shrugged. "By association, you do."

I glared at him. "Not the point I'm trying to make. I managed to get you in a picture. I wasn't trying to. I had no idea you were there." I sighed heavily, my head falling back against the seat. "Now they know what you look like. That you're with me."

Mill's face remained passive.

"Roxy said that this meant *war*, Mill. And that girl is crazy. She hated me from the moment she met me."

"She didn't know that you were a human until you bled, did she?" His gaze flashed to the gash on my arm, and I tried to cover it again with my shirt. Then he shook his head. "Cassie ... she knows you're a human now."

I groaned. "Which means that Draven could catch wind of the fact that I'm human too ..."

Mill shook his head. "I don't think so. They hate Draven, don't they?"

"Yeah, but they probably hate me more now, since I killed Benjy. Wouldn't telling Draven be a chance to get revenge?"

"That's three vampires you've killed now," Mill said. "Three kills under your belt. They aren't going to take that lightly."

"Thanks, I needed something else to worry about."

"You don't get it," he said. "You're not some weak-kneed human cattle to them now, like you would have been if they discovered what you were when you first met them. They're going to see you as a threat. They'll be cautious of you. I don't know of any human in recent history who's killed so many vamps and lived to talk about it."

Mill ripped a clean piece of his shirt off and slid over to where I was sitting. My heart beat faster as he gingerly tied the shirt sleeve around my bleeding arm. He tied a neat knot to hold it in place.

"The other thing that you have to consider is that they don't know for sure that you weren't a spy of Draven's, right? If there's even a small chance of that, they won't go running to him with the news that you're human. That'd be like signing their own death warrants."

I swallowed hard. My blood was already starting to stain through the makeshift bandage. "Why would they think Draven would work with a human?"

"Plenty of vampires have loyal pets. Didn't you see that in Miami?"

I flinched. "So you think I'm safe?"

Mill's gaze hardened. "Safe ... is probably not the best word." His stare intensified. "As long as you're with me, though, you're the safest you can be."

I was still uneasy. None of what he was saying made me feel any better about it. The one advantage I had, the secret of my humanity, had been ripped from me. Quite literally. With nasty, sharp, vampire fingernails.

"Mill ..." I said, touching my injured arm. "Why did you

come for me?"

The question hung in the air. Mill was a vampire, and one of only two who I'd met who I'd consider "nice." Every other vampire I'd known of acted like the ones at the club in Miami tonight; people were only good for wearing collars and being a sustainable source of food.

Mill cleared his throat. "Because you asked?"

I gasped as the phone on my lap vibrated, and then cried out in pain as the movement jostled my ribs. Xandra was calling.

I ignored it. I had told her I was back, didn't I?

"I don't buy that for a second," I replied. "That is the dumbest excuse I've ever heard."

"After all this time, after all the help I've given you, you're still suspicious of me," Mill said, crossing his arms over his chest.

I scowled. "Um, how could I not be? You're a freaking vampire. I'm human. At some point, this relationship is going to get tested." I held up my arm, a fresh wave of the acrid, metallic stench of blood filling the air. "Worse than this."

Mill's eyes followed my arm.

"I don't get it. Why are vamps such cast-iron jerkheads, but you're so nice? I mean, did gypsies curse you with a soul?"

"They're called the Romani—and no. It's not that simple," he said.

Finally, I was getting something out of him. At the same time, it seemed like every time I thought I understood something, new information cropped up that sent my head spinning.

"Vampires are no more cut and dry than humans are," Mill said, frowning as he looked out of the dark, tinted window. "When someone becomes a vampire, their basic needs remain the same. Survival. A place to live. Finding something to eat. The curse that is thrust upon a vampire is just that: a curse. Everything in us, our very humanity, is wrenched away in service of bloodlust. The desire to feed on people makes it easy to forget the humanity of those we feed upon. In a way … if you're going to eat live humans, you have to forget what it means to be human. In order the live the way vampires do, to embrace the call, to feed on people ... you can't see them as like yourself. You have to be ... superior. Otherwise ..." He shook his head.

He paused. The limo slowed and stopped for a red light, then picked up speed again.

"Some vampires go utterly mad after their conversion. They have these urges to feed on people, and they try to contain it. But the longer a vampire goes without feeding, the more insatiable their desires become, and the harder it is to fight. I've seen an entire busload of people killed because a vampire tried to fight their own nature too long."

I stared at him, open-mouthed.

"Others are power-drunk. They were weak as humans, and then find that they're the strongest creatures in the world. They don't care that they're irredeemable. All they care about is getting their next fix."

Charlie's easy smile flashed across my mind's eye, his story about the human he had almost killed fresh in my mind. Hadn't Benjy said something about him using? Was he just blood drunk?

Mill turned his weighted gaze on me. "Still others are slaves. They have no hope. They simply exist. They don't experience any joy in their choices, but they're addicted to them all the same."

I frowned. "Which one are you?"

The limo slowed to a stop.

"We're here," Mill said. Not an answer. I stared for a moment ... but none was coming.

"Pull around the corner to the house two down from here," I said. The driver complied, bringing us up in front of Laura's house.

Hopefully ... we'd made it before Roxy and Ivan had.

Chapter 25

"Why are we here?" Mill asked.

I pointed to the upper window of the dark house. "This is Laura's house. Roxy was going to come here and turn her tonight. She seemed to think that their numbers were too low after Charlie's death."

"She was talking about it openly?" Mill said. He grimaced. "She really had no idea that you were human. You certainly played your part well." I pulled open my phone, found Laura's number, and hit the call button. It rang and rang … finally she picked up.

"Hullo?" said a sleepy voice on the other end.

"Laura? It's Cassie."

"Cassie?" she repeated, her voice clearing. "Why are you calling me at—four in the morning?"

"Sorry, but it's important. Can you come outside and meet me?"

"No. I can't. Are you crazy? What are you doing up right now?"

"Laura, I need you to come out here and get in the limo."

"Limo?" She sounded like she was going to choke on her blankets, her voice was so sleepy.

"Yes, limo," I said. "Listen to me. You are in danger."

"What?" She was fully awake now, though she kept her voice quiet.

"Those vamps are coming to get you, to turn you," I said. "Don't ask me how I know that—it's too long of a story, and honestly I don't want to talk about it. Just get down here."

"I ..." Laura murmured. "I don't think I should."

"Are you freaking kidding me right now?"

"It's just ... my parents are out of town. I'm here by myself."

"You were home alone all night? And you didn't tell me?" I asked. "Laura, that is a big no-no when vampires are after you."

"You said I'd be safe at home." Yeah, she was waking up now; there was a little fire in her reply.

"You were." I heaved a sigh. "But if I hadn't been with them all night, you'd probably be one of them by now."

"Wait, you were *with* them?"

"I said I didn't want to talk about it."

"You were the one that brought it up!"

Mill nodded.

"Not helping," I mouthed, pointing a finger at him.

"You told me not to leave the house," Laura said. "Now all of the sudden it's okay for me to come out? At night? What if a vampire gets to me?"

"What if they burn your house down with you in it?" I countered.

BANG BANG BANG! I nearly jumped out of my skin. Jerking round to the window where the thumps had come from—

"Gregory ..." I muttered, clutching my hand over my heart that was beating wildly. He peered in through the window, an almost crazed look on his face.

"What about Gregory?" Laura asked on the other end of the phone.

I reached over and grimaced at the pain in my arm as I threw open the limo door, drawing the scent of low tide and salty air inside. Gregory was standing out in the night, fully dressed, his face pale and eyes wide behind his glasses.

"What are you doing here?" I asked. "Why are you up at this hour?"

"You called me," Laura answered.

"Not you, Laura," I snapped.

"Laura?" Gregory asked. "Is that her on the phone?"

I glared up at him. "Why did you just knock on the window of some weird limo?"

Gregory's brow furrowed. "I got your text," he said. "And since the fashion squad wasn't trying to break down Laura's door, I assumed it must be you."

Mill turned to me. "This kid is involved too?"

Gregory's eyes moved from me to Mill, who was sitting in the seat beside me. One of his eyebrows arched. "Who's the Cro-Magnon man?"

Mill's eyes darkened.

"Cassie, who are you talking to?" Laura called from phone earpiece.

"Just get down here, Laura. You're safe—for now. But not for long." I looked up. Gregory was hesitating outside the limo door.

"Oh, get in," I said. "It's not smart to talk where other people could overhear us."

"Wait—" Mill started, but Gregory had already climbed inside.

"Fine," Laura said. "I'll be down in a second."

"Don't dawdle," I replied, moving aside to make room for Gregory. "Bye." I hung up the phone.

"So, what, are you stalking Laura now?" I snapped at Gregory when he was in and the door closed behind him.

"You should talk," Gregory said, "sitting outside her house at four in the morning."

"I'm trying to protect her," I said. "What are you doing?"

"The same, but less stylishly," he said, crossing his arms as he looked around the limo. His face blanked as he noticed my arm, his defensiveness melting. "Cassie ... you're bleeding."

"I'm aware of that," I said.

He shifted his gaze to Mill, giving him a firm once-over. "Did he do that to you?"

The two stared at each other suspiciously.

"No," I said. "Another vampire did that."

"Another—wait—"

Laura appeared, shrouded in moonlight and wearing a

comical—given the circumstances—fluffy pink bathrobe. Her hair looked perfect despite just getting out of bed, as though she'd styled it before setting foot out of the house. I leaned across and opened the door for her as she approached, a look of trepidation on her face. She was walking jerkily, eyes darting—searching for vampires. Well, bad news, Laura: you're about to meet one.

"Get in," I said, low.

Laura crossed the last of the distance to the limo on quick feet. She slipped in beside me, Gregory having begrudgingly moved over opposite Mill .

In one trembling hand, I caught sight of an improvised stake: a piece of broken trellis.

"It smells like rust and cologne …" Laura mumbled. Her eyes widened when she saw Gregory. "What are you doing here?" And she continued her visual sweep of the car. "And who's this guy? Why is he covered in tar?"

"Vampire," I said dryly. Their expressions twisted in horror.

"But he's a *good* vampire," I said, taking only the smallest amount of pleasure in seeing Gregory lean away from Mill nervously.

"I won't eat you," Mill said to Laura. "Either of you," he added with a quick glance at Gregory.

For some reason, Laura did not relax.

"Wait, was he one of the ones who helped you with Byron?" Gregory said, his eyes narrowing.

"Sort of," I answered.

"Can someone please tell me what is going on here?" Laura asked, wrapping her arms tighter around herself.

"Not now," I said. "Later, yes—but we need to get away from here, before Roxy and Ivan show up."

Laura asked weakly, "Roxy and Ivan?"

"Your stalker friends." I added, "What remains of them, anyway."

"Where are we going?" Gregory asked.

Mill looked from me to Laura. "I have a place that we can go."

"Where?" I asked.

He knocked on the window to the driver, and when the smoky glass divider slid down, gave him an address.

"That's on the Bay," Gregory said.

"I know." Mill turned his dark eyes on me, and I tried not to make too much of it. "It's my place."

Chapter 26

Mill lived in a place that I did not expect: along the eastern side of the city, across the street from the longest sidewalk in the world that ran all the way down the southern peninsula of the city, and was nestled right alongside Tampa Bay. It was a modern building with clean lines, more windows than cement stretching up into the sky.

The limo dropped us off near the front door. The lobby was of the swank city type; crystal chandeliers, marble floors, and blooming orchids on every surface. Mill moved swiftly through, even as the man behind the front desk waved at him. Gregory, Laura and I followed awkwardly, awed and out of place.

After a thoroughly uncomfortable and silent elevator ride, we stopped at the tenth floor. Mill stepped out and walked all the way down to the end of the hall. He unlocked the door and flicked a light switch, then stood aside to let us in.

We stepped into a large rounded foyer, with doors on either side, that led down a hall into a large, open room with a back wall of windows. There were pine hardwood floors, whitewashed walls, and an intricate glass lantern that hung over our heads.

"Whoa …" Gregory whispered, sliding his hands into his pockets.

Mill didn't react; he locked the door, which had three seriously large locks, and then walked farther inside, turning on more lights.

I followed.

The apartment smelled of leather and bergamot, and I realized with a start that I noticed that scent every time Mill was around.

Mill was a minimalist. He had two sparsely decorated bookshelves on either side of the flat screen television. There was only one painting on the wall across from the windows; a series of rolling hills in the dawn light. A black leather sectional took up most of the living room, wrapping around a plain glass coffee table with a stack of books about architecture, and rested on top of a plain grey rug.

I saw what looked like open Japanese paper doors, and a sleek desk in the dark room beyond. The kitchen was also dark, but I saw high-end metal everything, and what looked like a wine fridge, glowing blue.

I shuddered. Wine coolers and I were not on good terms.

Mill set his keys in what looked like a bowl made of real silver on a simple wooden buffet table beneath the painting. Beside it rested a small dragon carved from a bright green stone. Was that actual jade?

How long had it taken to acquire these things?

"I bet the view from here is amazing in the daytime," Laura said breathlessly, stepping toward the windows like a fly drawn to a bug zapper.

I glanced at Mill. "Yeah. How do you deal with all the sunlight in a place full of windows?"

Mill reached for a small remote on the buffet table. He pressed a small red button, and blinds that had been nearly invisible above the windows slid slowly down over them like drooping eyelids.

"Ah."

"For a safe house, this is pretty impressive," Gregory said, giving the room an appreciative glance around. I wasn't sure I wanted to admit it out loud, but yeah. It was a pretty cool place. And nothing like Byron's, which had been over the top fancy, full of gold and velvet. A good thing, really—I couldn't bear to be here otherwise.

"Cassie, come with me," Mill said. "I'll get you some clean clothes."

Right—my bloody arm. I knew that he had insisted it didn't bother him, but there had to be a limit to his tolerance.

I hesitantly followed him down another hall. He stepped into the last room on the left, another clean, simple affair fragranced with that pleasant air of leather and bergamot. The bed had a dark headboard, pristine white down comforter, and a half a dozen pillows. Two white end tables were adorned with simple glass-bottomed lamps. A little bonsai tree, which seemed to be flourishing, sat atop the dresser.

"Why do you have a bed in your room?" I asked him. "I mean ... you don't sleep, right?"

He pulled a black t-shirt out of the dresser and tossed it at me. I caught the faint scent of bergamot again.

Mill opened another drawer. "Of course we sleep."

I watched his face carefully, which remained blank. He tossed a pair of pajama bottoms at me, red plaid.

He straightened and pointed at another door along the wall. "The bathroom is in there. Go ahead and get cleaned up. I'll get a bandage for your arm."

And with that, he left the room.

The bathroom was modern and clean, also entirely white. Marble sink, glass-walled shower, and yet another tall window spanning from floor to ceiling.

I set to work peeling the bloody fabric from my skin. It was hard to believe that only been a few hours before I had been getting dressed in my best clubbing attire – well, mine and Xandra's – to just see what these vampires were about, maybe get some insight into their plans.

I tossed my filthy clothes into the sink and turned on the hot water.

I glanced at the shower and debated hopping in, but the idea of being so vulnerable nearly made me vomit in the sink. Instead, I used my bare hands to wipe as much of the dried blood, both mine and Mill's, off me before pulling the t-shirt and pajama bottoms on.

The hot water was soothing, easing some of the tension in my muscles. The bar of soap frothed nicely and smelled of lemon and lavender.

My own blood washed out easily, but the vampire blood was another story. It looked like tar and dried like tar. I scrubbed at it with the flowery-scented soap, but to no avail. The stake tangled with the pile of clothes. I fished it out, rinsed it off, then dried it and tied my hair into a bun, pushing the stake through to secure it. At this point, I didn't want to be without one ever again.

Feeling significantly better, not to mention cleaner, I bundled my damp clothes and padded back out into the living room.

I found Mill sitting on the couch with a book in his hands. He had changed and looked good as new. A package of bandages rested on the arm of the couch beside him.

Gregory and Laura were whispering to each other, though not quietly. Gregory's shoulders were hunched up to his ears, and Laura's lips were pressed tightly together. Gregory looked like he was trying to console Laura. Laura didn't seem to want any of it. She kept flinching as if she expected to get attacked by Mill.

Mill pretended they didn't exist. He looked up when I stepped into the room.

"Feel free to leave your clothes over there," he said, pointing to one of the barstools. "Vampire blood is hard to get out. I'll take care of it for you. But first, let's get you bandaged up."

He moved over on the couch, making room for me to sit right beside him. He turned to Gregory and Laura. "You can sit too, you know."

Laura laughed nervously, playing with her hair. Gregory just hesitated.

"It's okay," I said.

That seemed to stir them to life. They slowly made their way around the couch to join us.

"So, what now?" I asked Mill as he started to unwrap the bandage.

Mill's fingers were like ice against my skin as he began to wrap the gauze around my arm. It was almost pleasant against the low burn of my clotting wound—almost. Because, helpful to me or not, he was still a vampire—and I was his natural prey.

"Well, we're safe from the remaining two for now," Mill said when at last the bandage was secure. "They may know my face, but they'll have no luck finding me or where I live. And they didn't follow us." He examined my arm carefully to ensure he had covered it well. "Besides, if you're right and they want war, they aren't going to skip town after what just happened."

"What do you mean, 'remaining two'?" Gregory asked, his eyes fixed on my arm in Mill's grasp.

"Well," I launched into a modified version of the night's events. I didn't give all of the details of my fight with Benjy, or how disgusting the fight between Mill and Ivan had been, but by the time I was finished, both Gregory and Laura's faces had turned ghostly white.

"So they were coming to …" Laura gulped. "Turn me?" She stumbled over the word.

Gregory's jaw tightened. "Why tonight?"

"Didn't you hear my story?" I asked. "We cut their little posse in half tonight and gave Roxy a holy facial."

"Yeah, but …" Gregory said, "what was turning Laura tonight going to accomplish?"

Mill stepped in. "Roxy is an emotionally driven creature. She was grieving the loss of one of her lovers—"

"Wait, *lover*?" I asked.

Mill turned his eyes patiently onto me. "Why else would she have reacted that way?"

I swallowed hard. Maybe he was right. And I'd just thought this was her gang. Maybe there was more at work here than I had thought. I tried to push it out of my mind.

Laura made a whimpering sound. "I don't want to become part of this kinky Instaphoto vampire gang."

"No, you really don't," Mill said. "Nobody does. It's why they have to turn humans to get members. No self-respecting vampire wants to be part of what they've got going on."

"This whole thing is just so bizarre," Gregory continued. "Fascinating, almost." Laura shot him a murderous look.

"I said 'almost,' didn't I?" He cleared his throat. "What do we do now? It's not like we can just live here at Mill's condo forever, as nice as it is."

Mill nodded, and then suddenly straightened.

"Get to the spare bedroom," he whispered, rising to his feet so fast it didn't register in my brain.

"What?" Laura whispered, grabbing Gregory's arm tightly.

Gregory's face flushed.

"Door on the right," Mill whispered, gesturing for us to move. "Quickly. Quickly!"

"Mill, what is it?" I breathed as Gregory and Laura stumbled past the coffee table. "It's not them, is it?"

"No," he replied. "Go. I'll explain later."

I hesitated, but his gaze was ominous and forceful. "Go!"

I turned and hurried down the hall after Gregory and Laura.

We slipped into the room and closed the door behind us, falling into darkness.

"Shh," I whispered to Gregory and Laura—their breathing, hers in particular, was loud, rapid.

I pressed my ear to the crack between the door and the frame. Mill's footsteps hurried across the condo. The sound of locks being unfastened ...

"Hello, my love," said a woman's voice, smooth as fresh-poured blood. "I was wondering if you were home. I brought you something ... fresh." She rattled a plastic bag.

A blood bag.

Mill had a girlfriend.

A vampire girlfriend.

Chapter 27

"Who is it?" Laura hissed.

I nearly jumped out of my skin. I'd forgotten she was there for a second.

"Some woman," I said. "Hold on."

I returned my ear to the door. The new vampire woman was talking animatedly.

"... didn't answer my calls? I thought we'd talked about that," she was saying.

"Kate," I heard Mill reply, sounding particularly drained. "I'm sorry. I had other things to take care of tonight."

"I'm not an idiot, you know," the Kate replied nastily. Heels clacked against the hardwood floor, growing louder—she was coming this way. "That's what you say every time you ignore my calls. Pretty soon I'm going to start to feel like maybe your heart just isn't in this, Mill."

My heart hammered against my chest, worried that she might walk straight into the room.

But Kate's steps stopped short—still in the living room, I thought.

"You've got that look again, like you're guilty about something," Kate snapped. "Did you make a kill and not invite me? You've been seeing other women again? Sneaking around?" She sounded less upset as she ticked off the possible offenses, like going on a human hunt without her was the height of betrayal. My head whirled at that.

"No, Kate," Mill said, a touch of annoyance in his tone. "I

haven't done any of that. Shouldn't surprise me you'd accuse me, though; they say the guilty see their crimes reflected back every time they look at someone ..."

Kate did not respond to that for a long moment, but when she did, it was a doozy. "Whose clothes are those?"

Oops.

A weight like lead formed in the pit of my stomach.

"You want to tell me why you're here this close to morning?" Mill countered.

"You want to tell me what you were doing all night where I couldn't reach you?"

"Not exactly, no," Mill answered.

"Fine," she said. "Then maybe you'll be interested in the latest piece of gossip I heard this evening."

She took a moment to pause dramatically.

"There's talk of war, Mill."

War? That was what Roxy had said. The weight in my stomach increased.

"Why?" Mill asked.

Kate laughed, a loud and sharp sound that made me grit my teeth. "Apparently, another vampire was murdered tonight. In Miami."

My blood went cold, my knees weakened. How in the world did the news travel that fast? Charlie's body was still warm in the grave, figuratively speaking.

"Cassie, what's she saying?" Gregory whispered.

I shushed him again.

"Varycas, the Lord of Miami, seems to think that it was a territorial move orchestrated by Draven himself. The kill happened in one of his nightclubs, in full view of everyone. The guy got slipped holy water." There was disdain in Kate's voice. "Stupid. And messy."

"How do they know it wasn't one of Varycas's?" Mill asked. "Some internal turf move?"

"Because they arrived with that bunch from Tampa. You know the ones—that Instaphoto girl Roxy, with her little harem—"

"I really don't want to be part of a harem," Laura said, paling, her head against the door next to me.

"The one who died was a favorite for the girls," Kate said. She snorted. "He was pretty hot."

I could see Mill's face in my head, his face darkening, his jaw clenching.

"This is all rumors?" he asked, his voice tight.

"It's all true. I have my sources," Kate purred.

"You were with Draven tonight, weren't you?"

"Maybe I was, maybe I wasn't," she answered playfully, annoyingly.

"Nice."

"I don't have to tell you if you're not going to tell me where you've been or who you're with," Kate said. "Draven's pissed, regardless. A Tampa vampire going down in Miami? And stirring talk about reprisals? You know how touchy Lords can be."

"Why does Varycas care if it was one of our vampires that died?"

"Because it was his club, and the cops got called. It'll probably even make the papers. Varycas may allow a little more bleedover into the human world than Draven, but he's not going to sit still for that much attention. He's already howling at Draven. And Draven wants to smooth it over, so he's sending envoys over there." Kate giggled, and I wanted to slap her.

"He's asked if I'd be one of them."

"You want to get in the middle of this?"

"Why not?" Kate's voice was snippy again. "Can you imagine if a full-blown territorial war between the southern and western Florida vamps broke out?" She cackled with surprising glee, and I wondered if maybe witches were real too. I questioned Draven's judgment in choice of envoys, because it sounded to me like Kate was way more excited by war than peace.

"You seem pleased by the thought of bloodshed," Mill said. Creepy that he read my mind.

"It's been too long since we've had a good war," Kate went on. "Everyone has been so ... soft. Well-behaved. We're vampires. Bloodshed is what we do."

"We don't drink our own," Mill retorted. "We're civilized.

We follow the rules. We make peace. It's what makes us better than the humans."

"You mean it makes things better *for* the humans," Kate said. "Peace and quiet, yawn. Hiding our true faces ... our true *teeth*?"

He made a sound like a grunt of displeasure, and I imagined her all up on him.

It made my stomach drop.

"You always have had a soft spot for the bleeders," Kate said. "We should be free to be who we are, do what we need to do. Those humans can exist and do whatever they want during the day. But the night ..." She snickered. "It's ours."

"You can't even see what kind of insanity that would lead to?" Mill's voice was quiet, almost humble.

"I don't care. I think that Varycas has the right idea, allowing his vampires in his territory to bring their human pets out in public. Draven could learn a thing or two from him."

"We have to maintain the divide between our societies. We have to keep to the shadows," Mill said, almost desperately. "If we don't—if the humans marshal all they have against us ... We will lose everything."

"Mill, when are you going to realize ... they couldn't hope to stand against us." She laughed. "You're not one of them, you know. Your heart stopped beating a long time ago."

"Kate, if a war breaks out, it is not going to go the way you think."

Kate just laughed. "More of them will die than us just by population size alone. Besides, we can rebuild our numbers from the wealth of warm bodies in this city. What are they going to do?"

I slumped against the wall, sliding down to the floor.

Quiet whimpering floated through the darkness—Laura.

"It's okay ..." Gregory whispered soothingly.

I understood. The idea of a war breaking out in our city was terrifying. Given the vampires' speed, strength, and insatiable desire for blood, the only logical conclusion was that Tampa was going to turn into a graveyard.

"Don't be so mopey, Mill," Kate said. "The humans have

had it coming for some time."

We've had it coming, have we? I reached up and touched the stake in my hair. I'd killed three vampires myself. And I was a seemingly helpless teenage girl.

Maybe more vampires were like Mill, who actually cared about humans, or were trying to maintain their own humanity. Maybe they would convince Draven that a war with an outrageous amount of human causalities would be a bad idea.

A prickling, burning sensation started at the back of my throat.

Who was I kidding? There was no way that the vampires would look out for humans over their own interests.

"I'm going to have to talk to Draven," Mill said quietly.

"Why would he listen to you about anything?" Kate asked.

"I ..." Mill started. "I don't know. But this is spiraling out of control too quickly. Someone needs to stop it."

Kate scoffed. "Do what you want, Mill. But regardless of what you do tonight, this war is going to happen. It might not be today, or tomorrow, but it is going to happen. And then the innocents will die, and blood will flow." She dropped her voice so that I had to strain to hear her. "We'll be like kings and queens. I don't know why you fight it."

The words echoed in my mind.

Blood will flow.

What had I done?

Chapter 28

Mill shooed his girlfriend out of his apartment less than ten minutes later. They had switched to arguing in hushed voices too soft for me to understand, and when he finally threw open the door to the spare bedroom, all three of us shrieked, terrified that it was Kate.

"Sorry," Mill said, but didn't stay to see if we were all right. He walked back out to the living room.

"Mill," I started, clambering to my feet and hurrying out after him. I left Gregory to help Laura off the floor. "Mill, hold on."

I didn't like the way that my voice trembled.

Mill was standing in front of the windows, his arms folded across his chest.

"Mill?" I asked cautiously, taking a step toward him.

"I'm sorry you had to hear that," he said, not turning to look at me.

"I—" I was at a loss for what to say. My mind was whirling so fast that it felt like the room around me was spinning. Maybe it was the loss of blood. I decided to sit down on the couch.

"How ..." I tried again. "How are we going to fix this?"

Mill remained silent.

"And another thing—" I started again, anger flaring from nowhere. "You never told me that you had a psycho girlfriend." Mill shot me a sidelong glare, but still did not answer.

Did he ever intend to tell me that he was dating some vamp witch who hated humans?

My cheeks flushed. Who was I to think that I was close enough with Mill to know that sort of personal information? He might have saved me a couple of times, but that didn't mean we were friends.

My hands tightened into fists in my lap.

Get a grip, Cassie. There are more important things to worry about right now. Like a vampire war that could be starting under our noses.

How were we going to fix this?

"This is all my fault ..." I mumbled. "If I hadn't tried to track down Roxy and her gang, none of this would have happened."

Mill sighed heavily and turned around to face me.

My heart sank as I gestured up at him. "You wouldn't have felt the need to come bail me out of my own stupid decisions, and Charlie and Benjy would both still be alive ..."

Tears stung the corners of my eyes. "And you wouldn't be on their hit list, and they wouldn't know that I was a human." I barked a laugh. "There is no way that any of this could have gone any worse."

"Thirsty McGee could have made things worse," Gregory said. "If she had found out we were here ..."

Mill shook his head, glaring at the coffee table. "That's why I had you hide. Let's just say that she isn't known for her gentleness."

Gregory cocked his head at Mill. "Are you sure you're not considering joining Roxy's kink squad?"

Mill just gave him a glare.

"That much was obvious from her attitude," I sniffed. Laura's hands were trembling. It looked like Gregory's arm around her waist was all that was keeping her upright.

"I was so scared she was going to find us ... and eat me ..." she whimpered.

"Nothing was going to happen to you while I was here," Mill said firmly. "And I won't leave you to be eaten by her either."

"Very reassuring," I muttered sarcastically.

"You're starting to sound like Kate," Mill said through

gritted teeth.

"What do you see in her, anyway?" I said, my eyes narrowing.

"Not the time, Cassie," Gregory snapped. "We sort of have bigger problems right now. Like a bunch of vampires fighting and killing each other?"

"He's right," Mill said.

I wasn't going to let him off that easily, but decided to hold my tongue for now.

"So what do we do?" I asked. "If this other Lord in Miami wants a war, how can we possibly stop him?"

"We don't have to stop him," Mill said. "We have to stop whoever Draven is sending after Ivan and Roxy."

I sat up straighter. "What? I didn't hear her say anything about those two."

"That's because she didn't mention their names," Mill went on. "Before I chased her out of here, she told me that Draven was sending a sweep team after the rest of the group that the murdered vampire had arrived in Miami with. Draven wants them for questioning."

"Wait" I said, getting to my feet. "'Sweep team'? Does that means he's going to ... y'know ..." I ran a finger over my throat.

"No," Mill said. "They'll be taken to him alive, where they'll be compelled to tell him all about the girl who killed Theo, and me, her helper, of course."

"If Roxy tells Draven about me, about what happened—" I sunk back down onto the couch again. "Mill ... Draven will know I'm human."

"And it won't take very much for Draven to realize that the two of us are connected, especially after Roxy saw us leave together." He looked pained. "I don't exactly want Draven finding out that I've been working against him. Couple that with the fact that I was the one who killed a vampire in Varycas's territory ... well, I'll be in trouble."

I scrubbed my hands over my face. This wasn't happening. This couldn't be happening.

"Then we have to get to Roxy and Ivan first," I said, hope piercing the despair washing over me like a monsoon. "If we can find them, we can—"

But I was unable to finish my thought. Nothing I could think of would work. There was no guarantee we could overpower them. And apologizing and asking to be allies against Draven would never work.

"What's done is done," Mill said.

My temper flared. "So you're just giving up?"

"I didn't say that," Mill said. "All I meant is that the damage has been done with Roxy and Ivan."

"What do you think they'll do?" I asked. "Honestly?"

"Do you think they'll run to Lord Draven?" Gregory asked.

"That'd be suicide," Mill replied, waving his hand dismissively. "Slow suicide, at least. But Draven is in control of a very large territory. He'll do all he can to track them down and find out everything they know about what happened tonight."

He started to pace back and forth across the living room, running his hands through his short, dark hair.

"Draven has spies, obviously, and they're all over the place. He learned what happened in Miami tonight from them, even if it's only fragments. That's why he sent the sweep team after Roxy and Ivan. He'll capture them and torture them—"

"Torture?" Laura whispered.

Mill spared her only a momentary glance. "—to find out why they've done what they've done, and everything they know. If they disliked him as much as they said they did … it's not going to end well for them."

He paused, his jaw clenching.

"Draven does not take well to things going awry in his territory. That's why he mentioned envoys, and peace talks. He'll do everything he can to hush it all up, dispose of the problems, no matter how many vampires he has to kill. What Kate doesn't understand is that peace is much more profitable than war for vampires. Draven will do all he can to keep the peace, because peace means he remains in power."

"All of this is making my head hurt," Gregory moaned, removing his glasses and rubbing his eyes with his thumb and forefinger.

"So we need to catch that sweep team," I said. "Follow them—especially if they have a lead to where Roxy and Ivan will be."

Though what we were going to do once we found them, I had no idea.

Mill considered—and sighed.

"I can't think of anything better to do at the moment," he said. His shoulders slumped with exhaustion. He looked over at Gregory and Laura. "You'll have to come with us. It won't be safe for you here if Kate comes back to spend daylight here."

I felt a twinge of frustration. "She has full run of the place then?"

"Not the time," Mill snapped at me. Then his gaze softened. "When we find them, we have to kill Roxy and Ivan."

"Kill them?" Gregory asked, hushed.

"It's the only way to keep them quiet," Mill said.

"Wait, Mill, I didn't think—"

"Cassie, it's either this ... or Draven finds out everything."

My breath caught in my throat. When he put it so starkly ... he definitely had a point. Even if I hated it.

"Besides," he continued. "If we succeed ... they won't be a bother to Laura anymore after this."

I looked over at Laura, whose eyes were as round as saucers. She was clutching Gregory's arm as if they were sitting side by side in a movie theater, watching a horror film.

If only. How had things ended up spiraling so madly out of control in just one night? No more than eight hours ago, the plan had been to recon the vamps and find out how to protect Laura. Now it was seek and destroy. War loomed on the horizon, endangering not just my life, not just Mill's, but all maybe every human in Tampa's.

And in order to stop it ... we had to keep Lord Draven finding out the truth about me and Mill.

Chapter 29

"How are we going to find this sweep squad?"

We had squeezed ourselves into the back of a silver Mercedes town car that Mill had called for. Laura had been reluctant to leave, even with the knowledge that Kate could come back. There were dark circles under her eyes, and her perfect hair was starting to tangle.

A strange impulse passed over me. I wanted to hug the poor girl and tell her that everything was going to be okay.

"Hey, you still have your stake?" I asked her gently as we stood on the sidewalk, waiting for the car to show up.

She nodded, her bottom lip quivering.

Mill, who was sitting up front with the smartly dressed driver, did not answer my question.

"Mill!"

He started, and then glanced over his shoulder.

"What?"

"How are we going to find the sweepers?" Gregory asked for me.

I had to admire Gregory's courage through all of this. His brow had stayed one long, wrinkled line since he had climbed into the limo outside of Laura's house. All of his usual good humor had seemingly been leeched from him.

I couldn't hate him for wanting to protect Laura. But as I looked down and saw their fingers knotted together tightly on the seat between them, I couldn't help but feel a little jealous. Laura may not have wanted Gregory as anything more than a hand to squeeze for moral support, but Gregory took it in stride, circumstantial or not. He was a rock for her when she desperately needed one.

A wave of loneliness swept over me. I hadn't had that when I was dealing with Byron.

I *still* didn't have it, even surrounded by people and Mill.

"It won't be hard," Mill said. "I contacted one of the other vampires I know who's in Draven's inner circle. He's the closest I have to a double agent. I know the names of the vampires on the team, and where they're headed."

"Convenient," I said.

"It pays to make friends with those in power, Cassandra," Mill said.

Cassandra? I pressed my lips together in annoyance.

"So where are we going?" Gregory asked.

"To an old neighborhood in eastern Tampa," Mill replied, checking the map on his phone. "Just down the road here." And he craned his neck to be able to look up at the tall buildings rushing by us.

I wished I had more than one stake on me. Laura had never used one, and Gregory was defenseless. And on top of that, Mill was injured. I mean, I was too, but Mill was definitely going to be the one carrying us here.

"Okay, slow down," Mill whispered, peering out the window.

The driver obeyed.

We found ourselves in a seedy neighborhood, where windows were boarded up, vines climbed up walls, and half the streetlights were out.

The driver stopped outside of an old theater, which was advertising movies that had released months before.

"That's that discount movie theater, isn't it? The one where that guy got shot last summer?" Gregory asked, leaning across Laura to look out my window.

"Oh, great," Laura said. She would have melted into the seat if she could have.

"Someone died here?" I said, noticing that more than a third of the lightbulbs around the matinee signs were out.

"But they have movies for like, two bucks," Gregory

replied.

"We should have left you at home," I snapped at him.

The driver pulled into the narrow drive leading around the back of the building, where the parking lot was.

"Kill the lights," Mill said before we reached the corner of the building. We cruised around the corner, deadly silent, blending into the darkness—

A black cargo van was parked under one of the few streetlights still capable of function around the back of the theater, its angles hard and stark in the glow from directly overhead.

"There's the sweep team," Mill said. "Turn the engine off."

Again, the driver complied.

As we watched, the door to the van slid open, and figures dressed in black stepped out, one after another.

"They look like an actual SWAT team ..." Gregory whispered.

He was right. They wore black from head to foot, and masks over their faces. For a moment I had mistook their attire for a ninja's—but as they stepped more fully into the light, I realized that the dark wrappings around their heads were, in fact, helmets.

"Why are they wearing those?" Gregory asked. "The helmets."

"It's to protect them from the sunlight, right?" I said, glancing to Mill for affirmation. "If they have to work during the day? That way they don't spontaneously combust."

His eyes were squinting with concentration, but he nodded. "Yep," he grunted in reply. "They don't like to do it—but if they have to ..."

"But the sun is still a while off," I said.

"Shh," Mill said, holding his hand up.

The group was moving quietly to the back door of the theater.

Why would Roxy and Ivan be here? I would have expected them to have gone to another trendy club or penthouse.

Well, duh, Cassie. That would be the first places I would look if I were Draven. Maybe Roxy wasn't quite as much of an airhead as I thought she was.

"Okay, you three," Mill said, turning on us as if we were children. "Stay put."

"Mill, wait—"

He spared me a glance, but his face was set, and he didn't respond. Opening the door in a fluid, vampire-quick motion, he slipped out and closed it, somehow without a sound.

He was going to fight them.

He was going to kill them.

… or at least try to, anyway. Laura's hand found mine, squeezed. I resisted for a second, but eventually let her wrap her fingers around the back of my hand.

"He'll be okay …" she whispered.

My throat burned. I didn't reply.

Mill crossed the parking lot in less than a second, and we watched as he stood tall, wound up, and socked the first helmeted vampire right in the middle of his back.

The vampire went flying into the van with a loud crash, crumpling the metal door like tinfoil—there went the surprise factor. A wooden stake stuck out of his chest.

I gasped, and Laura's hand tightened around mine painfully.

The element of surprise totally gone, the other five vampires in the sweep team whirled on Mill. They unsheathed what looked like police batons from their belts—only these were longer, with wooden tips sharpened to points—

Stakes. My chest tightened in terror as the tableau held for a fraction of a second—

Then the sweep team surged at Mill.

He ducked out of the way of punches flying faster than my eyes could follow, and side kicked another vampire right in the hip, causing him to topple over. In a flash, he shoved the next one down with his shoulder—

Holy smokes.

Mill was a fantastic fighter.

They weren't slowing, though. They all were getting back on their feet, moving so fast back to the circle around Mill that it was like they were teleporting.

It was insanity. Mill was throwing moves around like he

was straight out of *The Matrix.*

Another vampire hit the ground, screaming, a stake the length of my arm through his neck. Blood like oil spread out beneath him.

"Doesn't he have a huge hole in his stomach?" Gregory asked, astonished.

"He does," I said. My voice sounded distant. My hand was turning clammy in Laura's.

They all moved so quickly, it was hard to tell who was landing hits and who was taking them.

Byron had moved as quickly as these vamps did, he'd been an amateur compared to Mill and these ninja SWAT superhumans. Laura gasped as Mill took a hit to the leg, making him cry out in pain.

"No!" I cried, leaning closer to the window, my breathing coming in sharp, painful bursts.

Time seemed to slow as I watched Mill take another hit, this time right in the gut.

It was like I had been punched, too.

"I can't just sit here and watch this," I said. Beads of sweat were forming on my face.

"Cassie, no, that's crazy!" Laura said, pulling my hand toward her. I had almost forgotten she was holding onto me.

"You'll get hurt!" Gregory said. Killed, more likely. But Mill was out there—he was being overpowered—

I pulled the stake from my hair, threw open the car door, and made to jump out.

"Cassie! You can't seriously be thinking about getting involved in that!" Gregory hollered, leaning across Laura to grab the back of my shirt.

It was like my head was not attached to my body. I looked around at Mill, who was lost behind the sweep team.

"Miss Howell?"

I started at the formality, and looked up to see the driver of the car looking back at me with startlingly green eyes.

"Hey, I remember you!" I said. "You're the driver Iona sent out to meet me a few months ago!"

The driver smiled and tipped his chauffeur hat to me. "William Lockwood. I usually go by Lockwood."

He nodded toward the trunk of the car.

"If you want to help, you'll need more than that little stake you're carrying."

"What do you—"

There was a distinct click, and the trunk popped open.

Swallowing the bile rising in my throat, I nodded at Lockwood, and stepped out of the car.

Chapter 30

I wasn't sure what I was expecting in the trunk of the car, but it was not what I found. What lay before me was a full-blown arsenal, arranged in metal cases lined with black foam that smelled brand new. There were wooden stakes by the dozen, ranging from the size of pencils, all the way to several inches in diameter. The leather bag filled to the brim with little glass vials couldn't be anything other than holy water, and the sealed glass bottles with the strong smell of gasoline indicated Molotov cocktails. Crosses were carefully wrapped in cloth, and there were also candles, and several changes of clothes.

My mouth went dry as I looked through it all.

Mill was a vampire, and yet, here he was, carrying around enough vampire-slaying gear to kill every vampire in the Tampa territory.

What the heck did he get up to in his free time?

I looked up over the car as I heard another crunch of metal, and saw Mill standing on top of the van now, clutching his side.

The vamps in the SWAT gear were circling the van, lions circling their trapped prey.

"Come on, come on …" I whispered under my breath.

If Mill died on me, I was going to …

Where did that sudden surge of desperate hope come from? Why was I so invested in his wellbeing?

You idiot, Cassie. He bent over backward to help you. He flew all the way to Miami because you texted him and told him you were in trouble.

I couldn't see his face clearly, but the way he was holding his stomach showed that he was not doing well.

He'd surged in so confidently—but now he hung back, reluctant to press any further.

Were we in way over our heads?

I couldn't move. My feet were glued to the spot, my legs heavy as lead.

And then—

A strangled gasp escaped my mouth as Mill suddenly launched himself off the van toward the brick wall of the theater a good twenty feet away. He then immediately jumped off the wall again, using it as a springboard, and flung himself at one of the vamps.

He collided with the SWAT vamp with a howl, and I clasped my hands over my mouth as Mill ripped the vamp's helmet off, grabbed either side of his face, and then snapped his neck.

The vamp crumpled. Even hurt, Mill was—strong. A lot stronger than I would have thought, even seeing him in action once tonight already. Heat flushed my face. Whether out of fear or ... something else, I didn't know.

Move it, Cassie!

There was a flurry of motion that was too fast for me to follow, but the hits were coming harder and faster.

As the fight continued, my body grew more and more tense. My back ached, my breathing came in shallow bursts.

Mill was incredible. He managed to keep himself outside of the group, never leaving his back exposed for very long. It was almost as if he knew where the next hit was coming from.

The vamp that had had his neck snapped was stirring, trying to lift himself up off the ground. He dragged himself forward—toward Mill, I realized too late, who was engaged with another, taller SWAT vamp, lost in a flurry of blows—

I moved to cry out—

The vamp on the floor latched onto Mill's ankle with his teeth. Mill roared with pain. Black blood gushed out of him from between the vampire's teeth, the sulfurous odor intensifying in the night. One of the remaining sweep team members had clambered onto the van—whether to escape, or press an advantage, I didn't know. It chose the latter option now though: seeing Mill momentarily incapacitated, it leapt down onto him, landing heavily. Mill staggered under its weight and fell. My desperation peaked—and my feet unglued themselves. Reaching into the trunk, I snatched up as many vials of holy water as I could carry—hooked a jagged left around the car, ready to throw—

I froze.

What if one of the vials hit Mill? What if it hurt him more, with his open wounds?

What if it leached inside of him, set him alight, the way it had when Charlie ingested it?

But I had to do something. I was starting to get desperate. I had to get close. I had to help.

I couldn't let him take the fall for me. I couldn't.

And what if the vials didn't land close enough? All it was going to do was draw their attention to me, and inadvertently, to Gregory and Laura, a couple of sitting ducks in the car.

I might have been armed to the teeth, but my reflexes were pathetic next to these vampires. Mill could get hurt. And burning him would do me no good …

Damn it, Cassie, move!

I glanced desperately at the trunk, hoping for some alternative, something I could use that would be more precise than these holy water vials, like grenades launched haphazardly into the night—

Gregory and Laura shrieked, the sound barely muted by the limo's windows.

I looked up—

My chest constricted.

Mill, who was clutching the front of a vamp's throat, was hit upside the head, hard. So hard that it sent him flying into the brick wall of the theater.

He wasn't moving.

And while he was down, one of the other vampires sauntered up to him, wooden police baton in hand. He slowly wound up and brought it down right across Mill's chest.

Chapter 31

I froze. All I could do was stare at the place where Mill was sprawled, the remaining four vamps closing in on him.

It wasn't happening. No. It couldn't be. Mill had to be okay. He had to be.

Everything moved in slow motion—my heart beating in my chest, its mad frenzy turned to a sedate *thud … thud*; the vampires, advancing on Mill—and me, carried on feet that moved of their own accord. The vampires didn't see me. Didn't hear me.

There was nothing left to lose. There was nothing left to do.

Mill had done so much to help me. He had protected me, saved my life at least three times. He deserved the same kind of loyalty from me.

One of the vamps lifted his boot, used his toe to turn Mill's head to look into the face of his killers.

Anger flared in my chest.

"I'm coming," I murmured.

Serene calm came over me, pushing fear to the far corners of my mind. My trembling fingers steadied, and I took great, deep breaths. The entire world seemed to be in perfect focus, like my eyes had dilated the way a cat's did as it set upon its prey. Oxygen swept through me, fueling my body. Adrenaline coursed through my blood too, heightening my reactions, banishing the looming fatigue of another long, unending night.

I had killed three vampires. All of them had terrified me.

All of them had tried to kill me. Closer I came.

This near, I could see that the armor covered the sweep team's chests, backs, and shoulders.

The streetlight glinted off of the glass vials in my hand. I had one chance—and one chance only.

I closed so that I was only feet from the nearest vampire, the last to approach the downed form of Mill ...

And then, stake extended, I sprang—

And plunged it right into his armpit, where his armor didn't quite cover. I angled it hard down, aiming for the heart.

Black, stinging blood sprayed out over my hand, causing it to slip on the stake.

The vampire roared, spun. A hand grabbed for the stake—

I lost my grip, fell backward.

He wheeled around and stared at me, astonished, enraged—and scared.

He was dying. And he knew it.

Slumping down, he hit the ground hard. Still, his clawed fingers worked at the stake embedded in his flesh—but they were weak, and his frantic gripping was become an imprecise flailing motion—

He coughed, dark clots of blackness. Skin melting ... Not dead, yet—but down for the count.

Unfortunately—

The others in the sweep team had rounded on me.

Dark glares surveyed me.

The lead resettled his grip upon his baton-stake.

"You two stay with him," he said, nodding at Mill, who was struggling to get to his feet. "I'll deal with the backup."

Backup? Oh, come on. He couldn't be that dumb, could he? He approached—and removed his helmet.

"Out of breath, are we?" the vampire asked with a cruel grin, his fangs protruding.

I gritted my teeth.

"This is going to be easy," he said. Then he rushed me.

I dove out of the way, sort of expecting it. This wasn't the first vampire to have underestimated me.

Thank you, Byron, for teaching me to flinch away from you. So much so that I was able to dodge out of the way of this new friend I was making. But it definitely came at a cost.

The pain from my ribs was starting to rear its ugly head. Whatever adrenaline had been surging through me had done its job, leaving me exhausted, dizzy, and slow.

The vampire laughed at me as I heard Mill throw himself at another one of the vampires from somewhere near the wall.

He didn't even give me a chance to catch my breath. Again, he seemingly teleported in front of me.

I took a deep breath and launched a punch at his face with my now free hand.

Pain flared through my knuckles from the impact. I recoiled, agonized. Great. Not only had I broken some ribs, but now I was pretty sure that one of my fingers was broken, too.

All I had left were my vials of holy water.

The vampire stalked toward me as I floundered backward, tripping over one of the cement parking spot markers. He flung a punch—

I barely ducked it, wheezing. Damn it, why was I so out of shape? Why hadn't I taken a self-defense class or something in the past few months?

I staggered backward, mere inches from the fist that sailed again through the air at my face—My back hit something solid. Why was I always getting backed into corners?

The vampire came to a halt right in front of me, his helmet still held casually under his arm.

He was confident he was going to win this fight. Out of the corner of my eye, I could see Mill, struggling to keep the other two off of him. He was only fighting with one hand, the other wrapped tightly around his middle—but he was still fighting, damn it.

"Cassie!" he shouted. "Cassie, run!"

The other vampire in front of me just laughed—and then punched the wall just beside my right ear.

The other hand shot out—and pinned me by my neck in a hold one notch lower than a choke against the wall. I'd screamed at the punch. But his ice-cold fingers locking around my neck stilled it in my throat.

"*CASSIE!*" Mill roared.

"Now, now," the vampire said coolly, bending his face lower to mine. His breath was fetid, coppery, like old blood … and cold, like the lungs that produced it. "There's no need to run off yet. I'm hungry. It's going to be a long shift. I could use an easy meal."

I spluttered, unable to force words out of my lips.

"I'll let my friends take care of your master over there," the vampire cooed. "Then we'll see about taking you back to Lord Draven for a little chat."

My face contorted into a pathetic pout.

The vampire threw his head back and laughed, an evil cackle that chilled my skin. But it was the opportunity I was waiting for.

Before he could move, I snatched one of my holy water vials free—and smashed it open over his mouth.

The effect was instant. His laughter turned to a scream as flames erupted. Releasing me on instinct alone, he screeched, backpedaling, clutching at his skin in horror. But it was too late: enough of the holy water had gone down his throat. Now he was burning from the inside out. And like an ice sculpture, he was going to succumb to it—quickly.

I darted away as he thrashed, contorting wildly, skin turning to black goo—

Arms grabbed me, and I shrieked, fighting and shoving to get away.

"Cassie, it's okay!" Mill's voice, I realized.

The fight left me. I fell to my knees, hard, in a street a million miles away from here.

Mill crouched over me. Concern—no, *fear*—lit his eyes, and blood dripped from his fingers.

"It's all right," he said, still more gently.

I threw my arms around his neck, the tears coming hot and fresh. They spilled over my cheeks and onto his shoulder.

"Cass …" he whispered.

It took him a second or two, but he wrapped his arms around me too. It didn't take long for the last vampire's screams to die out. His collapsing body, reeking of rot and burnt tar, quenched the flames. When I looked up, all that was left of him was a black, scorched lump, and his helmet and stake baton, lying a few feet away.

"They're …" I mumbled, looking around wildly. "They're gone?"

"Yes," Mill said, trying to steady me, his hands gripping my shoulders. "Yes, they're gone."

Chapter 32

Footsteps thudded against the parking lot, and I looked up to see Laura and Gregory running over to us, hand in hand.

"That was crazy!" Gregory cried. "Cassie, are you okay?"

I nodded. It was a glum nod, which was stupid—I should've been elated to have gotten out of this alive, to have saved Mill too. But no longer powered by adrenaline, I was tired—and I saw just how stupid I'd been in running out there.

"If this gets any worse, we're going to have to take you to the hospital in a matchbox," Gregory said.

Laura quivered at his side. Again, I got the feeling she was standing only because Gregory's arm around her waist was supporting her.

"Can we go?" she asked, looking around. "What if more come?"

Mill seemed to have the same idea. "They won't find anything when they get here. Other than the van and their gear. We'll be long gone by then."

He refused to look at me as he stood and starting lumbering toward the car.

My lips quirked into a frown. Was he mad at me?

Since Mill's help had now expired, it was Gregory who stooped to help me to my feet. I lurched along at his side. He didn't proffer his arm, which was probably a good thing because it would have been rude not to accept it, but he stuck close.

"What's wrong?" Mill asked, looking over his shoulder at me from the front passenger seat when I climbed in and Laura worked the buckle for me.

"I think I broke my finger," I said.

Mill heaved a sigh—an almost over-dramatic one which was totally more Kate's fare, but alien coming from him. "Cassie, you aren't a vampire. You can't do the stuff you were out there doing. You're going to get yourself killed."

"I know I'm not a vampire," I snapped back. "But you would have died if I hadn't intervened."

"Did it cross your mind that I was doing it to keep you safe?"

"You dying would not have kept me safe. All it would have done was kill all of the rest of us."

"I had it under control," Mill said, turning back around. He added, after another huff, "Don't be such an idiot in future."

I suppressed a snarl.

"I thought you were amazing," Laura said. If she meant it, she didn't sound it—more like she was testing the waters, trying to find amicable ground for us to meet at. "Both of you."

"Well, I don't know if I would call what Cassie was doing as fighting," Gregory said. "She was kind of just ... flailing."

"Hey!" I rounded on Gregory, my broken finger pointed at his face. I groaned. Habit. "I *meant* to pour that holy water down his throat."

"That could have gone south, Cassie," Mill said darkly.

"Isn't that what learning to fight is all about?" I asked.

"Guys, can't we just be thankful that we all survived?" Gregory asked hopefully. "I mean, it was crazy what happened, and also sort of awesome—" He recoiled slightly as Mill glared at him "—but we're safe! And we got away! And now there's no sweep team to, uh ... sweep up the bad guys. Who are still out there."

"Yeah, let's just be thankful for what we've accomplished," Laura said.

"No!" both Mill and I growled at the same time.

Laura and Gregory looked back and forth between themselves. "They're arguing like a couple," Gregory whispered.

Laura punched him in the shoulder.

Oh, he did *not* go there. Did he not realize how ridiculous that sounded? Like I would date Mill. He was probably a million years old or something. And that scowling face he always made—

I was glad he was alive, for sure. But that didn't mean I *liked* him or anything. Plenty of people ran out in the face of danger to rescue others, right? That's what fire fighters did, and it wasn't always because there were *feelings* involved.

"So what do we do now?" Gregory asked.

"Well, now the trail runs cold," Mill said. "If Roxy and Ivan are smart, they'll leave town."

"Why?" I asked, the anger in me deflating at the possibility of their escape. All this work, and we'd missed them?

"They'll have heard the rumors," said Mill. "The vampire community in Tampa is not big. Word will travel fast. Now that the sweep team is out of the way? They'll have the time to bail out."

"So this means we go back to HQ and make a nifty suspects board with push pins and string tying our clues together?" Gregory asked.

Mill, Laura, and I stared at him blankly.

"What? Have you guys never watched a detective show?"

The theme song from *Pretty Little Liars* broke the awkward silence. My phone. Where was my phone?

I discovered it wedged between the seats, but just missed the call. Xandra. And not just the one call either—over the course of the night, she'd called over a dozen times, and sent twice as many texts.

"What the …?" Gregory asked, seeing the messages and missed calls over my shoulder.

"Something's not right …" I muttered, scrolling through her texts. They started out frantic, and escalated pretty quickly to sheer panic, and then … the same message, over and over again:

Call. Or else.

"Something is definitely wrong," I said, going to call her back.

"Wait," Mill said. "It could be a trap."

But I had already hit the dial button.

It rang once. Twice.

Before the third ring, she answered.

"Xandra, I'm so sorry. I am fine. I'm alive, it's okay. You don't have to worry. I'm fine."

The bottom of my stomach dropped when a voice answered that didn't belong to Xandra.

"Glad to hear it, new best friend." Roxy. I yanked the phone from my ear and hit the speakerphone button. Tried, anyway—in my rising terror, I missed the first time.

"—would have been crushed if something had happened to you," Roxy was saying. "Because, you see … I have your little friend here. What did you call her? Xandra?"

I heard a muffled scream of protest, and then a loud crash.

"Shut her up, will you, Ivan?"

I stared in horror—at Gregory, who was pale and wide-eyed too—but I saw nothing—only the image of my parents again, in the wine cellar at Byron's place—only now it was Xandra, and she had two vampires looming over her, even wilder cards than Byron had been.

"Where—" I stammered. "How did you—" *Know about Xandra,* I meant to finish. She hadn't been involved in any of this—so how …?

"It's pretty simple," Roxy replied. "She showed up at the airport to look for you. Apparently she got an urgent text from her bestie telling her she was on her way to Miami." She laughed again. "Poor thing. She came all the way out here to help you only to be caught by the security crew … and then handed over to me."

My heart constricted, my throat tight.

"You must think you're so clever, *Elizabeth,*" Roxy sneered, "getting away from me. But that doesn't matter. Not anymore. You can't run forever, little girl. You've shown some real guts tonight by trying to be one of us. Seriously. I almost believed you. Someone should give you an Oscar."

"What do you want, Roxy?" I asked.

"Oh, come on, you haven't figured it out yet? Okay, it's getting close to sunup, so let me cut to the chase. I want to make a deal with you." A pause. "See? I can be reasonable.

Violence isn't always the answer, you know." I knew right then exactly what the deal was—knew it just as Mill did, his hands tightening on the seat, threatening to gouge the leather-covered seats.

Mine tightened too, on my phone, my knuckles bone white.

"You want to see your friend again, Elizabeth? Bring that pretty Laura girl and yourself, right now, and meet me. I know you've got her. Purple hair here told me you're friends, that you're *helping her.*" That prompted a loud round of mocking in the background, Roxy just cackling with amusement.

Laura sucked in a sharp, panicked breath. Tears burned her eyes, utter terror written on her face.

Gregory squeezed her hand.

I closed my eyes tightly, willing the entire thing, the entire night, to have been nothing more than a bad dream left over from all of my Byron PTSD.

Xandra, my best and only real friend, was in danger because of me. Why hadn't I thought about her? Why had I been so senseless as to think that she wouldn't be in danger?

What was I going to do if I was too late? What if . . .

"We're outside Lord Draven's, by the way."

There was a mutual shudder of fear inside the car.

"Let me make your decision easier," Roxy said when I didn't respond. "Either you bring yourself and that Laura girl here with you, or I give Xandra over to Lord Draven, and let him do what he wants with her. Sound fair?"

She snickered, and I heard Ivan laugh out loud in the background.

Xandra's voice cried out again in anguish and was quickly stifled.

I was going to be sick.

"I'll see you soon," Roxy said in a sickly sweet voice. "Best Friend."

Chapter 33

"Damn her!" I lashed out. I punched the door three times in quick succession, and immediately regretted it. Hand throbbing, I whimpered and let my head fall back onto the seat.

"Lockwood?" Mill asked quietly.

"Yes, sir."

"Let's go back to my place."

"No!" I grabbed the back of Mill's seat and shook it. "No." My mouth was dry. My head spun. "I just ... need a minute to think."

Lockwood turned down a side street and put the car in park.

The slow, repetitive clicking of the turning signal grated on my nerves, making it even harder to think clearly.

Think, Cassie.

"Cassie ..." Mill started.

We had lost. For one second, one blissful, perfect second, I thought we had a chance. I had survived a fight with vampires again. Mill had made it out. We had Laura, who was safe and sound. And Gregory, who had gotten himself involved when he really shouldn't have.

But Xandra. Snarky, sarcastic, loyal Xandra. *What were you thinking, girl? Why in the world did you try to take it into your own hands to try to rescue me?*

Gee, I wonder whose example she was following, trying to do some rescuing?

"It's not your fault," Laura murmured, putting her hand in mine.

"If I hadn't told her where I was, she'd still be safe at home ..."

"If it wasn't Xandra, Roxy would have found something else to hurt you with," Mill said. "You know that."

"But they don't know who I am," I protested. "They don't even know my real name."

"Doesn't matter," Mill said. "Even if it wasn't tonight, she would have found you eventually. If she's threatening to go to Draven ... he's got resources. Contacts. He'd track you down as soon as she told him you're human." He forced a weak smile. "But she hasn't—yet."

"Because she wants me to show up," I said.

"Yeah, what's up with that?" Gregory asked.

All three of us—four if you counted Lockwood and his green eyes—stared at him. Was he really that dense?

"Didn't you hear?" Laura asked. "She called Cassie 'best friend.' She wants to turn her." Laura looked at me. "She wants to turn both of us."

"But that'd mean she wants you as part of her gang," Gregory said, just rambling along, "which we already know is kind of like a harem—"

"Stop talking," I said, souring on him instantly. Laura looked at me out of the corner of her eye; I did not look back. There was no part of this that appealed to me. No offense, Laura.

"Roxy's feeling reckless, if she wants to do this outside Draven's place," Mill said. "She's arrogant, and therefore she'll be easier to beat."

Easy for him to say. He was a vampire. Even if he was bleeding all over the front seat, he had a better chance of winning in a fight against Roxy.

"For what it's worth, Cassie," Laura said quietly, "I'm grateful for everything you've done for me."

"I haven't done anything," I said, voice hoarse, "except make things worse. For all of us."

Xandra's cries echoed in my mind, and I squeezed my eyes shut against it.

"I have to go ..." I said softly. "I can't just leave Xandra there to—to die." The words caught in my throat.

I hadn't even wanted to get involved in all of this. When Gregory first came to me, I had laughed in his face. Who would want to get involved with vampires again?

Curse my conscience. The guilt ate away at me, and eventually made me give in. I didn't want someone else to go through what I went through. The perilous, overwhelming isolation, and the lack of support. Having to lie at every turn, knowing that no one would believe me.

All of it had been to save my own skin.

Enter Laura, and suddenly, I turned into the hero.

More like anti-hero. Reluctant, angry, a failure.

Byron had taken my parents. I hadn't hesitated to rescue them.

Roxy had taken my best friend. And here I was, paralyzed with fear, with four sets of eyes boring into me.

I'd never be able to live with myself if anything happened to Xandra, especially when it was in my power to help her. Her death would be on my hands. It would be my fault.

"You don't think that Roxy would hurt Xandra, do you?" I asked. "While we're waiting, I mean?"

Mill hesitated, and my stomach dropped. "I don't think she would," he said, after an eternity of a few seconds. "She's angry, yes. But she knows the only way that you'll play her little game is if you see Xandra alive, at when we go to meet them."

Xandra may have been an accidental friend, but she'd believed me when Byron was stalking me. She'd been there when I needed her. We'd come together after that, bonded, as though this vampire business had welded us together. And tonight, she had demonstrated the depth of her friendship by sneaking out in the middle of the night to go to the airport to try and find me.

Throat stinging, eyes burning, I took a shaky breath.

"You'd think this would get easier," I said. "Fighting vampires, I mean."

Laura watched me pensively. She'd have worry lines on her forehead for life after tonight.

"I know how scary all of this is," I said to her, my hand

tightening in hers. "I've never been so scared in my life, and I know you understand. The only thing that even comes close was when my parents caught me in a really nasty lie back when I was living in New York. It wasn't pretty. And I totally deserved their wrath."

"I totally understand," Laura said, tears leaving streaks down her pale face.

"I wish that was all I had to be afraid of right now ..." I said, scrubbing my eyes with the heel of my palms.

"You're crazy for going through with this," Gregory said. The streetlights outside were glinting off his glasses. "But ... I kinda get it now."

Mill made a sound like a growl deep in his throat.

"I understand that you want to help your friend, Cassie—" And the tone in his voice told me that I didn't want to hear what he was going to say. "But you should get out of this while you can." Uproar from the backseat—from all of us, Laura included, albeit in quieter, politer protestations.

"Do you seriously not care about this? About Xandra?" Gregory shouted. "It's because she's human, isn't it? She's just another casualty to you."

"You cannot honestly expect me to just—to walk out now!" I said. "She's my friend!"

"And Ivan is a destroyer," Mill answered, gesturing to his stomach. "Roxy has no mercy. She lost a lover tonight, remember?"

I opened my mouth—but Mill continued.

"I know your friend is in danger," he said, "but even if you win this—it's going to be on Draven's doorstep." He hung his head. "And honestly ... I don't know that we can win." He was holding himself, pained. "That sweep team ... they took a lot out of me. I'll be going into a fight with Ivan, and I'm not exactly a hundred percent here."

"I ... I don't care," I said. "I don't care whether you're going. I am *not* leaving my friend in the hands of these monsters."

Decision made. Again.

I was going to go, and I was going to fight.

Dawn was coming, and Roxy wanted to end it. My stake

had fallen into the footwell. I knelt over, picked it up gingerly, and then deftly slid it into my hair where it belonged.

"Let's end this," I said. Mill did not look happy, and for a long moment he watched me, imploring me with his eyes to reconsider.

I did not. And so, finally, he turned to Lockwood, and said flatly, "Drive."

Lockwood drove.

Chapter 34

I recognized the building before we even stopped in front of it. This building had been the place where my life had changed forever. Here was where I went from being a terrified human girl to a vampire slayer pretending to be undead. I'd played my part so well that Lord Draven himself had believed my story.

But if he didn't know the truth yet, he soon would. If Roxy had her way.

My hands wouldn't stop shaking as Lockwood pulled into the parking garage behind the condo.

This time, there was no long line of limos waiting to drop off or pick up vampire guests, no party in progress.

"It's almost six," Gregory said, glancing at his watch. "Not long until sunrise."

"I want you two to stay in the car," Mill said to Gregory and Laura. "With Lockwood. He'll get you out of here if things get hairy."

"What about Cassie?" Laura asked, eyeing me nervously.

"I'll protect her," Mill replied. Then he turned his eyes on me. "Are you ready?"

My ribs were good and bruised, if not broken, I'd cracked a finger, and cuts and scrapes covered my entire body. I was going to need a doctor at the end of all of this. Assuming Mom and Dad didn't kill me.

If I made it home again.

No. Not if. *When.*

But whatever state I was in, I was going to fight. So I said to Gregory and Laura, "Listen to Mill. We'll see you guys soon, okay?"

They both nodded at me, their eyes huge.

I didn't wait to hear a reply. If either tried to argue me out of it—well, we were here, on Lord Draven's doorstep, and I was about to risk everything.

Mill had clambered out. He was already digging through his gear in the trunk. He had a handful of holy water vials, and a few stakes poked out of his pocket. I joined him, re-examining the trunk's contents. Adding to the stake in my hair, I grabbed a few more, slipping them into my waist band. I wished I was wearing my jeans, but at least Mill's pajama bottoms were easier to move in.

I also took one of the last bottles of holy water, as well as a Molotov cocktail.

"Don't get into an up-close fight with them," Mill said. He placed a lighter in my hand and picked up a Molotov for himself. "You're injured."

"I know," I said.

Mill slammed the trunk closed.

I followed him back out to the street and the front of the condo—

Roxy's shrieking laugh echoed into the pre-dawn light, down the empty streets.

"There you are, Bestie," she said. She was walking down the sidewalk toward where Mill and I were standing.

Ivan was following close behind, and I gasped when I saw him supporting Xandra underneath her arms, bound and gagged with strips torn from a sheet.

"Xandra!" I shouted.

Mill put his arm out, stopping me from going any closer.

She stared at me with wide, horrified eyes, her bright blue hair tangled and askew. A cut on her forehead oozed blood, a smear of it across one eyebrow—where one of her captors had licked it, I realized with a sickening churn of my stomach.

Ivan tossed her aside as if she were a ragdoll, and she hit the sidewalk, hard.

"Your little friend here has been most amusing," Roxy said, hands on her slender hips. "Brave too, which I am sure you'll be happy to hear. Called us some names. Ivan didn't take it too well when she spat in his face, though."

She glanced over her shoulder at Xandra, who was struggling against her bonds, attempting to roll over. "That's how she got her that little souvenir on her face."

I pushed against Mill's arm, but he held me in place. My heart hammered against my chest.

"Let me go!"

"Stop," Mill hissed at me.

Okay. Charging stupidly into the vampires and their superior strength was probably not smart. Fair point to Mill. I changed tacks. "So you ran back to Draven with your tail between your legs, huh?" I shouted. Blood still surged in my ears, my vision turning red.

Roxy snickered. "I'm not an idiot, Elizabeth. Or should I say ... Cassie?"

My heart sank. She knew my real name.

"I take it by the looks of you that you caught up with our sweep team?" Roxy asked. "There was really no need. We already came here to turn ourselves in. Draven prizes knowledge above anything, and we knew that giving him the name of the vampire—I'm sorry, *human*—who killed Theo— well, it'd allow us to walk away scot-free."

Mill growled, and I gritted my teeth.

"Gotta admit, you fooled me. There was something mysterious about you, and it intrigued me." She glowered at me. "Angered me, sure. Lots of people do that on first blush, though. I thought you were different. Special. I guess that my gut was right, though; there was something off about you."

"Your buddies lapped it up," I said. "Benjy and Charlie especially. They just loved me. To death."

Hate flashed in her eyes, and her hands curled into fists. "How dare you speak their names."

"Why so sensitive?" I asked. "Did somebody die?"

Roxy snarled and started to move toward me, but Ivan grabbed her arm. "We have the advantage here," he said almost so low I missed it.

Roxy wrenched her wrist from his grip, and then turned her glossy gaze back onto me.

"You came crawling back to us," she said. "And I'm glad you made my job so easy. Once I get rid of your boyfriend—" she looked pointedly at Mill, "—I'll be taking you up to see Lord Draven. Giving you over to him as peace offering, you understand. Get back in his good graces. I hoped maybe it could go differently—maybe we'd turn you, that you'd see things my way, that we could be besties, but …" She shook her head. "It's not worth the risk, running with you."

"And to think you and your little gang were so excited to party with me earlier tonight," I said. "You were so brave. What happened to all of that talk about overthrowing Draven? About how much you hated him and his rules?"

"I'm smart enough to realize that staying on Draven's good side means protection, long life, and freedom. Anyone who thinks otherwise is just showing themselves as a fool."

"So you're scared?" I asked. "Afraid of an old man?"

"You have no idea what you talking about," Roxy snapped back. "Draven has more power than most vampires combined. He's lived a long time. He knows *everything.*"

She exhaled and pushed her hands away from herself as if to clear her way. "But that isn't why we're here," she said, her voice calmer. "It's time for you to pay for what you've done. You've caused so much trouble for us, Cassie. You've taken away … my dear ones." Her eyes flashed dangerously, and Roxy took a few steps toward us.

Mill's hand gripped my shoulder more tightly.

"Do you know what that means for you?" She smiled, but there was no joy in it. "War, Cassie. You have declared war on the vampires of Tampa." She threw back her head and laughed into the waning night.

I was glad she was as shallow as Mill had said she was, because while she was talking, I'd slowly pulled the lighter from my pocket, and unscrewed the Molotov cocktail bottle.

As she cackled, I flicked the lighter three times before the heat of the flame pressed against my hand. I heard the crackle of the flame as the fire took to the fabric tucked inside the bottle and pulled it from behind my back.

And then I chucked it into the air.

All of our eyes watched it sail through the air. Roxy's laugh died in her throat, and Xandra screamed against her gag.

The bottle soared past them and shattered against the sidewalk. Golden light flooded the street.

Missed.

Roxy shrieked another hearty laugh—and then started toward us.

Mill clenched his teeth. "Good try," he said—and then launched himself at Ivan.

Chapter 35

Their fight from the airport resumed with a vengeance. Dialed all the way to eleven, they were a flurry of blurred movements, thrown punches and kicks and grapples and clawing rakes that I could barely follow. Ivan and Mill went at each other like two men who'd never hated anyone more in their lives, totally focused on each other.

Which meant I had to deal with Roxy.

"So, *Bestie*," she said, taking a step toward me. A wide grin played on her face. "Looks like it's just you and me now."

I snuck a glance over at Xandra. She'd managed to prop herself up so that she could watch what was happening.

I had to get close to her. If I could reach her, then maybe—

"You do know that Ivan is the best fighter on my team, right?" She directed an appreciative look toward him. "He trained in Japan for almost a hundred years, honing his craft." Her lips pursed. "Though I must say, Mill is quite the fighter too. I wonder who he trained with."

We circled around each other slowly, a slowly rotating top.

Roxy's eyes glowed with murder. She intended to hurt me, and it wasn't just because she was a vampire and I was human.

No. This was personal. Like with Byron.

Circling, I knew she wouldn't let her guard down now, not even for an instant. That Molotov cocktail had been the last gap I'd find, the last opening she'd inadvertently give me.

So how in the hell was I going to win this?

Not alone. I needed Mill. Which meant he needed to beat Ivan … and I needed to stall.

"Valiant Cassie," Roxy murmured, about to spring. "Savior of humans. Friend of vampires who have turned their back on their brethren." Her face was growing clearer, and I wondered if my fear was giving me ultra-sharp vision, because of the adrenaline or whatnot.

But it wasn't that. The sky overhead was growing brighter, with the grey light of dawn bleeding into the black from below the horizon.

"You aren't going to win, Cassie," Roxy said. "Your friend over there is losing. I know you can see it, too."

She was right. I glanced at Mill, feeling like I must be watching a bad movie. It all felt so unreal. It had to be dream. He was flagging. Ivan pressing his advantage, and Mill was barely holding him off.

"Dawn may be coming, but you'll be dead before then," Roxy said. "How sad, to die after everything you fought so hard for tonight. You almost—kinda—made it."

I had fought for a lot last night. And even as the clouds overhead grew clearer, brighter by the minute, dawn wasn't coming fast enough.

And I wasn't going to see it.

I watched as if through a window as Roxy pulled her phone out of her pocket and snapped a few pictures of Mill and Ivan as they fought. She giggled, giving me a wide berth—because this taunting pause was not my chance, she was keeping well clear of me, and her reflexes were much faster than mine if I did try to make my move.

"Draven will want to see these. Seeing this murderer and traitor ripped to shreds will bring some joy into his sad little life," she said.

"And maybe spare you a staking," I added.

She glanced over her shoulder and grinned. "A worthy cause, you gotta admit."

Then she held up her phone high over her head, turned her back on me, and switched it over to selfie mode.

"Say cheese, girls!" Roxy cried. She winked at the camera,

laughing.

I could see my slight form in the corner, my hands at my side, clenched into fists. I was disgusting. Covered in black blood, my hair hanging in my face, and my clothing torn. Xandra was lying off to the side, peering up at the camera.

"I think I'll hashtag these 'bloodknights.' Or maybe even 'blooddays,'" Roxy said. "All my Instaphoto followers really love to see my little adventures. They'll be super interested about the fact that I managed to get my hands on two humans. But the after photos ..." She turned back to me, eyes glowing, her teeth showing. "Those, I probably won't be able to post."

She lowered her phone. "It's too bad I won't be able to turn you, Cassie. It would have been fun to make you my bestie slave for all eternity. Dress you up in cute outfits. Make you catch our human snacks." She sighed. "Maybe Draven will let me come and take you out for a night once in a while." She snickered. "If there's anything left of you to take out."

What would Draven to do me? Images of blood and collars and fangs and death filled my mind. Would he keep me as a pet? Or would he turn me himself?

I doubted he'd just kill me. He wouldn't be able to prove anything that way.

No, Draven was a politician. He'd use me as an example. Tour me around like a trophy.

I swallowed hard and pushed those thoughts out of my head.

"But your friend?" Roxy said, pointing at Xandra. "The police are going to find her body in a dumpster."

And like that, I snapped.

I reached into the pocket of my pants, grabbed a vial of holy water, tossed it—

And Roxy caught it effortlessly out of the air. She smirked at me. "Really? You didn't think that would work, did you?"

I glanced over at Xandra who was thrashing on the ground as if she were having a seizure. She was howling over her gag.

"Xandra!" I cried and took a step toward her.

And then Roxy was between us, appearing in a blur of motion.

She grinned. "Uh, uh, uh," she said, wagging a finger in my face.

I tried to peer over her shoulder and saw Xandra looking up at me. Her face was stained with tears, and I could see her desire to live. It was all there.

My heart constricted.

Roxy sneered, and turned her attention back to the fight between Mill and Ivan. Unable to match her speed or think of a way to fight her off, I did the same.

Mill tossed another punch. It was a slow, a great struggle. Pain pulled at his face, twisting his features.

Black, tarry, stinking blood stained the ground. His feet danced over it, dodging Ivan's blow—but it was too late, the ground too slick. Ivan sidelined the punch easily at the same moment as Mill *slipped*—

Then he drove his fist into Mill's gut again, right into the same spot he had wounded him earlier.

Time slowed. Mill teetered, doubling over.

A scream wrenched the air, and it wasn't until it was fading that I realized it had come out of my mouth.

Mill fell to the ground, landing on his knees, with a thud that echoed across the street.

He had lost.

I had lost.

It was over.

I was going to die.

Chapter 36

I remembered when I was really young, maybe no older than five or six, and my dad took me to a state park to see all of different colored leaves in the autumn. The air was crisp, the scent of a distant bonfire underlining it.

The most picturesque place in the park was on the path that followed the cliff alongside a river, which was fed by a lofty, wide waterfall in the distance. Rainbows danced in the spray. It was the most magical place I had ever been.

We were walking, hand in hand, and I was chewing on a candy apple, the caramel gluing my teeth together. Children were laughing, dogs barking, and the constant thrum of the crashing water filled the air.

Dad told me to stand up on a stone beside the river to get a picture. He said I was too cute, holding my apple with caramel on my nose and my hair in pigtails.

I stood on that rock, hoping he would get the picture soon so I could keep eating.

But the spray from the falls had coated the rock I stood on, making it slick. I tried to reposition my foot, but I slipped—

That fear that I felt, that paralyzing, heart-stopping terror as I plummeted from the rock and into the frigid, raging river stuck with me for my entire life. It was a frequent uninvited guest in my dreams, and up until I met Byron, that memory had been the most frightening moment of my life.

That falling feeling came back to me now, the complete loss of control, the inability to stop any of it.

Roxy was laughing maniacally as Mill tried to crawl away from Ivan, who kicked him in the side, knocking him over onto his face.

I clutched my chest, wishing I could rip my heart out. It was beating so hard now it was painful.

I pulled another bottle of holy water out of my pocket, unstopped it, and threw the open bottle as hard as I could at her.

The water bounced across her back and raced down it like rainwater.

She stopped laughing, and for a second, I thought it had hurt her.

She wheeled around, looking over her shoulder, and saw the vial on the ground, shattered. The water dripped onto the ground from the back of her jacket.

Looking up at me, she smirked. No damage done whatsoever, and—

I was out of holy water.

That left my stakes.

I tore one from my waist and charged across the distance to Roxy. I threw myself onto her back, screaming like a hyena, and wrapped my arms around her neck.

Roxy bucked like a bull, and I clung on even harder.

She wrapped her icy, stony fingers around my wrist, and pulled them away from her neck as if I were nothing more than a scarf.

My stomach clenched as she hurled me across the sidewalk, right near the road.

For the second time that night, I yelled in pain as my skin scraped against the hard ground. Blood streaked. Grit stung.

I rolled over and pushed myself up onto my hands, locating Roxy as quickly as I could.

She apparently didn't consider me a threat. Her back was to me again, and the stake I had been holding was on the ground at her feet. The others that had been tucked into my waistband were gone, apparently lost when I fell.

I was weaponless, aside from the stake in my hair. Of all of the weapons that filled Mill's trunk, I was down to my single, trusty stake.

History sure had a way of repeating itself, didn't it?

Roxy didn't care about me because she was far more interested in Mill and Ivan's fight, which was at its end. Ivan was just laughing now, going after Mill with cruelty, pushing the pain to him now that he'd beaten him.

"Mill ..." I whispered, my lip trembling.

Xandra cried out against her gag, and I looked over at her.

She nodded her head back toward the alley where we had parked.

I looked around but didn't see anything.

"I don't understand—"

Mill shrieked with pain, and tears spilled out of my eyes.

Mill was dying, and it was like I was dying with him.

Xandra cried again, and she was staring hard at the alleyway.

I followed her again and saw— "What the ...?"

Gregory and Laura appeared out of the shadows, both with stakes in hand, and Gregory had a cross held out in front of himself like a shield.

Ivan didn't see them, but Roxy did. She wheeled around and refocused her attention on me like the predator she was. Laura made to move toward me, but I held my hand out to her.

"No!" I said. "Help Mill!"

"But—"

"Go!" I said.

Roxy looked amused. "You can't be serious. This ... is your cavalry? A couple of humans?" Her eyes flashed as she recognized Laura. "At least you saved me the trouble of tracking her down."

And then Roxy was in front of me, her fingers wrapped tightly around my neck.

Searing pain bloomed in my head. I sputtered, coughed, and tried to draw a breath. But it didn't matter. I could only get a fraction of the oxygen I needed.

I grappled with her fingers, but they were like frigid iron on my neck.

Stars popped in my vision.

"Xan ... dra ..." I sputtered.

173

"Get used to not breathing," Roxy said quietly, rage filling her eyes as she squeezed even tighter. "You have no idea how much I want to just crush your throat right now …"

At that moment, part of me just hoped she would. I hoped that her hatred of me would push her over the edge and she'd just kill me once and for all. I couldn't bear watching Gregory or Laura die, let alone Xandra or Mill.

I didn't want any of it.

And with that thought, Roxy sent me flying through the air again.

I hit the ground—and she was on me again in a blur.

"I might have a little bite before Draven has his turn," she said, grinning. "After all, I doubt I'll get a chance to see what your blood tastes like after this."

Roxy was not a very big girl. She couldn't have been taller than me, and she certainly weighed less than I did.

Being a vampire definitely made her stronger than me, but not heavier.

Panting, I stopped struggling against her as she lowered her face to my neck. As soon as she felt my muscles relax, she relaxed too—and that was when I bucked her off of me. Thrusting my feet underneath her, I kicked out with all of my remaining strength, screaming at the pain in my ribs, sending her off of me, and into the street.

I rolled onto my side.

Roxy rose—

But she was out of luck. A car hurtled down the street, headlights flaring.

Its horn blared—

Too late.

The car struck Roxy square in the hip.

Her body careened through the air like a doll, spinning and seemingly weightless. She crashed into a bus stop—

The glass of the bus stop windows shattered, and the metal bent, crunching and crumpling beneath her as she landed.

The car screeched to a halt.

I stared—the driver too—world frozen—

Was she …?

"*ARGH!*"

174

The scream Roxy unleashed as she rose from the crumpled, ruined bus stop was like no other. It was pure, unbridled rage as its most powerful, a roar that went on and on into the pre-dawn light. Shards of glass rained off of her as she unfolded her body, apparently no worse for wear.

The driver swore, eyes wide. Then he threw the car into reverse and drove squealing back the way he'd come.

"Nice try," Roxy said, picking a piece of glass out of her hair and flicking it to the ground. "But you're going to have to do better than that."

Nothing was going to stop her.

Chapter 37

Roxy started toward me again, and I bolted away from her. I was getting farther and farther away from Mill and his fight, but it was going better. Either Laura or Gregory had managed to pour holy water onto Ivan, because he had stopped using one of his hands to fight with.

Now Gregory was circling around behind him with a stake, and Laura was standing off to the side, ready to throw more water.

Taking the only chance that I had, I dashed over to Xandra, still lying on the ground.

"Hey," I said, breathing heavily. "No, don't move. Let me try—"

"Cassie!" Xandra shouted, managing to displace the sheet gag enough to speak, her eyes wide as she stared behind me.

I was struck in the side again by Roxy's heeled boot. Pain seared through me from my broken ribs. I staggered to my feet—ran—

"Where do you think you're going?" Roxy stared after me for a second before giving chase.

The sky above was starting to turn pink, and I could see everything around me that wasn't bathed in the light from the lamp posts or Draven's building.

"Stop delaying the inevitable," Roxy called. She wasn't running after me. Which was good, because she could run me down in about a second flat.

I turned around and faced her, a solid twenty feet between

us. "You really think I'm just going to give up?"

Time was my friend once more. Or my enemy, depending how it all worked out. I'd needed time to help Mill. Gregory and Laura had come to the rescue. Now the sun was starting to rise. It wasn't far off, now. Reds and golds glowed from the east, as thin as ribbons along the horizon.

If I could keep her off of me just a little longer …

"I'm not an idiot, Cassie," Roxy said, face twisting. "I know what you're doing. You have no chance of seeing the sunrise again. You're done."

I was never a morning person. I'd rather stay awake until two in the morning and get up just before lunchtime.

But I promised myself then and there that I would wake up every morning for the rest of my days and watch the sunrise if I could just see this particular one.

"This night wasn't a total waste," I said—buying myself as much time as I could manage. "We took down two of your posse. They won't hurt anyone else, ever."

Roxy flashed toward me in a blur and her fingers snagged my wrist, tight.

Crap. Not yet.

I looked up at the sky, willing the sunrise to speed up. Come on, come on …

It was as if someone was holding the sun under the horizon, preventing it from cresting. Brilliant, bright streaks of pinks and oranges and yellows filled the sky, but no sunlight.

It wasn't enough.

Roxy's other hand knotted itself in my hair and she yanked back, then dragged me. My eyes screwed up and I grabbed onto her hand, trying to wrench it free, trying not to rip my hair from my scalp myself.

She was muttering something, but I couldn't hear her through the blood thumping in my ears. Down the street we went—I fought, legs kicking out—damn it, why couldn't the sun just burst from the horizon and end this?—but she pulled me like I weighed nothing, and though I thrust myself back, jerked, hoping to snap every strand of hair wrapped about her fingers, I couldn't—get—*free!* An engine roared: a more bass drone, less muted. Not a car, but a motorcycle.

177

It tore down the street—and screeched to a stop in front of Roxy.

The rider wore a black leather suit, from head to foot, their face hidden by a helmet that looked as if it was made out of the same metal that Draven's sweep team had had.

Roxy glared. "Who the—?"

The rider didn't answer in words.

They sent a leveling, devastating punch to Roxy's jaw that sent her reeling.

Roxy's grip on my hair evaporated as she crumpled to the ground. That punch had hit her harder than the car.

Panting, I stood up straight, staring in awe at the motorcycle driver.

The driver flicked the visor on the helmet up, and I caught a glimpse of sad, blue eyes, and a wisp of silvery blonde hair.

"Iona?" I asked, blinking, clutching my hair.

"You just couldn't stay out of this, could you?" Iona said.

The sun had finally crested over the horizon, bathing the street in golden beams of bright light.

Iona snapped her visor shut again, and reached down to where Roxy was lying, grabbed a fistful of her hair. Then, like Roxy had with me, she began to drag her out and into the street—toward the light of the sun.

"Hey, Roxy!" I called. "So ... not to go all 80's action movie on you, but ... wanna take a selfie?"

Roxy screeched with rage.

"No?" I asked. "I can hashtag it '#blooddays'?"

She fought Iona, but like me with her ... it didn't go so well. She writhed, but Iona's steely grip did not fail, and she pulled Roxy along helplessly.

I wheeled around to where Ivan and Mill had been fighting and saw a pile of black blood seeping out from an indistinguishable lump.

"Mill ..." I said, but saw Gregory and Laura a few feet away, still in the shadow of Draven's building, each with one of Mill's arms, pulling him across the lot back toward the alley as he sun crept along the street. The car had tinted windows. He'd be safe in there. They made it to the cover of shadows just as the sunlight drenched the alley entrance.

I heaved a sigh of relief and sank down onto the asphalt of the drive-up to the hotel. Faint sunlight touched Roxy's skin as Iona pulled her out, exposing her to daylight—and then her screams started for real. With one last heave, Iona threw her out into the middle of the road, effortless despite her even smaller frame.

The sunlight was paralyzing. Roxy couldn't right herself—could only writhe and shriek as the sun lit her in a faint glow—and her skin cracked, peeling and then disintegrating like dust.

I watched, side by side with Iona—enjoying it, not at all sickened with myself. Roxy deserved this—and I hoped it hurt as much as it sounded.

"That last line was terrible," Iona said finally, crossing her arms over her chest.

"What?" I said. "'Do you want to take a selfie with me'?"

"No," Iona said flat, "the #blooddays one. Though that one wasn't much better."

Roxy's screams turned to splutters, weakening as she disintegrated—until there was nothing left; only a pile of foul-smelling black tar turning to dust, shifted and dispelled by the morning breeze.

I was delirious. I couldn't believe that I was standing there, still living, my heart still beating.

And Roxy was dead.

"Want to come up with a hashtag?" I pressed Iona.

"Sure," she said.

"Really?"

"I'd go with 'no filter'."

I hesitated. "Wait. Are you talking about me or the picture?"

Iona gave me another small smirk, barely visible through the black visor, then turned to watch the last of Roxy's ashes disappear into the wind.

The sun was up. Roxy was gone. Gregory and Laura had been totally crazy somehow and beaten Ivan ... and Mill was safe.

It was over.

The longest night of my life was finally over.

Chapter 38

"Oh my—Xandra!"

I was an idiot. Such an idiot. How had I forgotten her? How had I—

"Relax, Cassie."

Iona, helmet firmly in place, pulled a knife from her back pocket and walked with me back down toward where Xandra lay.

"Xandra, I am so, so sorry—" I said, kneeling beside her as Iona started hacking away at the bonds around her wrists and legs. "It was just—Roxy and then the sun, and then Iona—"

"Cass, I get it," Xandra said. Her lips were cracked and her voice was hoarse. I wished I had water to give to her. "I'm just glad you didn't leave me here. Also, I'm pretty sure all of the blood is gone from my hands and feet." She gave Iona an apologetic look. "Sorry."

"The mention of blood is not going to send me into a frenzy," Iona said, pulling Xandra's wrists free.

After getting Xandra to her feet, I threw an arm around her and helped her to the car where I hoped everyone else would be waiting. Safely. In one piece.

Lockwood waited beside the car, in the shadow of the Draven's condo building. He tipped his hat to us as we approached and came to help me with Xandra.

"Who's—oh, I don't even care anymore," Xandra said as Lockwood effortlessly took the brunt of her weight.

"Where's everyone else?" I asked.

Lockwood spared me a glance and a smile. "In the car."

"Are they okay?"

"They're fine."

"And Mill?"

"He needs rest, but he'll be fine."

That dredged up another sigh of relief from me.

Lockwood opened the passenger door to the car and gently helped Xandra inside the car. Xandra gave me a questioning look, but as I went to follow Lockwood around the car, Iona stopped me.

"What?" I asked.

She looked at me through the tinted visor. "I still can't believe you chose to get involved in all of this."

My cheeks flushed, and I tried to swallow the lump in my throat.

"I should have listened to you," I said quietly. "Then none of this would have happened."

I couldn't see Iona's face, hidden behind the visor of her helmet. But I could see myself in a distorted reflection. Grimy, covered in dirt, and tear-stained. My hair was a wild mess, and my last resort stake still stuck out from my bun. I looked like a million bucks right now.

"You don't know how any of this would have unfolded if you had ignored it," Iona said. "Your friend could very well have been turned."

Wait ... was she ... complimenting me?

Iona nodded to the car behind me. "Because of you, she's safe and sound, and her pursuers are dead."

"No, that was thanks to *you*," I said. The image of Roxy being pulled by her own hair down to the street flashed across my mind. Maybe I should be more afraid of Iona than I have been. "How did you know I was here?"

Iona flicked open her visor, and I found that she was looking behind me again.

I turned to see the chauffeur walking back around the side of the car.

"Lockwood told you?" I asked.

She nodded. "He drives for a few of us. Said Mill had

called him for a favor, that he needed someone who would keep quiet. Lockwood's perfect for that. He's been working with me for a long time."

I looked back at Lockwood, and he leaned casually against the car, hands folded in front of himself. He smiled at me, green eyes sparkling knowingly.

"I'm glad Mill had the sense to call him," Iona went on. "He let me know that you'd gone to the theater. And after that, back here to Draven's hotel. If I hadn't been halfway across the state, I'd have been here sooner."

"What were you doing all the way on the other side of the state?"

Her eyes flashed. "Wondering how you managed to incite war talks between territories."

She peered at me through the visor. "He went to Miami?"

I filled her in about Charlie and how Mill had given him holy water.

Iona's pencil thin eyebrows arched, and she gave an appreciative nod. "Clever Mill. That was an effective way to deal with them, wasn't it? Right under their noses ..."

Her eyes narrowed again, and she gave me a peculiar look.

"It is interesting, though."

"What is?"

"Why Mill risked so much to protect you."

I blinked at her. So I wasn't the only one who thought it was weird that he'd done all that for me.

She didn't seem to have the answer to that though—and I suspected I wouldn't get it if I asked Mill. Instead, I asked, "Why'd you get involved? Why keep risking your neck to help me? Especially this time, when you warned me not to ... and I did anyway?"

"I already told you," Iona said. "I don't want you to end up like me."

"I get that, but—"

"No buts," Iona went on. She looked up at the sky over our heads. The sunlight couldn't reach us in the shadow of the building, but the bright Florida blue was a welcome canopy above. The clouds were like cotton candy, all pink and fluffy.

She sighed and put her hands on her hips.

"Look, Cassie. This whole thing—" she gestured between us "—is complicated. It has been from the very beginning. When Byron showed up in your life, I felt like it was my duty to help you. You were so stupid and knew absolutely nothing about this whole vampire world. You would have ended up like me if I hadn't stepped in."

"Hey, now," I said crossly. "Way to help me up and then kick me back down all in one. Very efficient."

She looked back up at me, and there was such sorrow in her stare. "You don't understand. I used to be just like you. My life was perfect for a seventeen-year-old. I had everything that I could have ever wanted. Everything. I had a family, and friends. I was smart. I had a future."

My heart ached. I wanted to hug the poor girl.

"I had a boyfriend at the time, too. He was a little older. But my mom liked him, and he was talking about getting me a ring …"

She held up her gloved hands to me.

"Now … I'm cold and untouchable, and things don't feel the same. After Byron … they never *were* the same …"

I wanted to ask her a million more questions, like what had happened to her parents, or her boyfriend. What had she told them? Had they just declared her missing and never found her? Because Byron had stepped into her life, because he had messed with her like he had tried to do with me, she'd had everything ripped away from her.

"All that I feel now is the craving," Iona said. "It's the only thing I really feel. There are still emotions, but … after he turned me? Everything was dampened but the hunger. Like someone put a plastic bag over the world. But people are vivid; you can smell the flavor of them." Good thing she was wearing a helmet, otherwise I might have worried for my neck.

Iona shook her head. "I still had the memories of my father laughing as he pushed me on the swing, the scent of cookies baking as my mother cleaned flour off the tip of my nose. Byron wanted me to forget the past, what came before. But I couldn't. I never have. They just faded from bright memories to desperately grey. How was I just supposed to forget all that when I hadn't chosen to be this way?"

It was awful. The entire thing. I didn't know what to say, or what to do. It hurt me, pained me as if the entire thing had happened to me. As if I had lost everything, too.

It often felt like I was about to. I had experienced and felt loss for things that I was still fortunate enough to have. But I had grieved for them, for those people, as if I had lost them.

She forced a laugh, nothing more than a sniff. "Vanity is a poor substitute for a heartbeat," she said quietly. "But it's what we're left with as vampires. The glory of self above all ..."

The lump in my throat subsided slightly.

"It's a miserable way to go through life. I wouldn't want you to have to live with that. Like I do." She glanced over my shoulder at the car, now running quietly, and sighed again. "You might just understand that on a visceral level now."

"I think I sort of do ..." I said, hoping my tone conveyed how deeply I did understand what she was talking about.

Iona slid her hands into the pockets of her leather jacket. "All set, Lockwood?"

He inclined his head. "Everyone is settled in and ready to go, Miss Iona."

Iona looked at me again. "I realize this is probably a waste of time to even say it, but ... this time, stay out of the vampire world, okay? For real."

Guilt made my cheeks grow hot again. "Yeah ..." I said weakly.

"But ... if the vampire world does come to call again, and sets its sights on one of your people, I know you'll throw what I'm saying right out the window. So. If that does happen, then please, call on me. Okay?" She snapped the visor down, her haunting eyes disappearing behind the black shade.

"Definitely," I said. "And Iona?"

She looked placidly at me.

"Thank you. For everything. Always."

I could hear the smile in her voice. It was such a rare thing. "It's what I'm here for, I guess." And she turned away.

"So ... no selfie together, then?" I asked.

Iona sighed, and reached into the pocket inside her jacket. I froze. She didn't think I was serious, was she?

She pulled whatever it was free, and then tossed it to me. Startled, I reached out to catch it, but it fumbled between my fingers, and then hit the ground below me with a metallic *clank*.

I stooped down to pick it up.

Round, made of a very light metal, it looked like a wide choker that came to a tapered point right below the collarbone. Something a knight might wear, or a person cosplaying.

"What's this?" I asked, turning it over in my hands.

"It's called a gorget," she said. "To protect your neck. If you're going to keep meddling in the affairs of vampires, you might want to make it a part of your ensemble."

I stared, weighing it. It was cool beneath my scraped and dirty fingers. "Um ... I really appreciate you looking out for me and all, but ..." I held it up between us. "A metal collar? It's freaking Florida. Hot? Sticky? Humidity in the range of being in the ocean itself?"

Iona shrugged as she turned and started back down the alley toward her bike out front. "You're tangling with vampires. Wear it. And learn to love the look of turtlenecks. And sweating. It burns calories."

She slipped around the corner, and was gone.

I gaped as I stared at the collar in my hands.

After everything I had been through tonight, maybe something like this wasn't such a bad idea after all.

Chapter 39

I got my first glimpse of the crew when I hopped in the front seat beside Xandra. It was a tight fit, but there was a middle seat between Lockwood's seat and the passenger door.

"Special installation," Lockwood said. "For larger parties such as this."

"And what a party it is," I said, looking around.

Xandra was sucking down what appeared to be her third water bottle. Gregory had an ice pack over one of his eyes, glasses tucked in the front pocket of his shirt. Laura was pale and wide-eyed, a tissue stuffed up one nostril.

Mill was lying with his head back, a clean shirt wadded up and pressed against his abdomen. Dark blood covered half of his face, the wound on his head starting to heal. He looked exhausted.

"How are you?" he asked, not even opening his eyes. Somehow I knew he was talking to me.

"I'm … fine," I said. "You?"

"Surviving," Mill said, crackling one eyelid. I saw a pupil looking at me.

"Where should we go?" Lockwood asked me, apparently since I was the only one of us coherent enough to give guidance.

Mill grunted something from the back seat, but I ignored him.

"We should get Mill home first, before the sun comes up

any more."

Lockwood nodded, and we started off down the golden-streaked road.

I turned around in my seat and stared at Mill. He looked as if he could be sleeping.

"That was pretty dumb, what you did back there," I said before I could stop myself. All of the worry and fear I had been feeling suddenly shifted to anger. "If Gregory and Laura hadn't come out to help you, all of this could have gone a lot differently."

Mill didn't answer. Out of guilt? Trying to tamp down his own anger?

"If something had happened to you ..." I started, but quickly recovered. "I don't know what I would have done. About any of this."

"Who was that woman on the motorcycle?" Mill asked.

I swallowed, but didn't think it was best to tell him. Not yet.

"She's just a friend."

"Has she been helping you this whole time?"

"No," I said. "She told me to stay out of it from the very beginning ..."

"It was like a movie," Gregory said. His words were somewhat mumbled; his bottom lip was swollen. "She showed up in the nick of time, right? Like *boom*, there she was. Rescue shows up just before the hero gets taken out."

"Except this is all real life," Mill grunted.

"How did you two take down Ivan?" I asked, turning to Laura and Gregory.

They exchanged glances. Laura decided to answer.

"Well, Gregory got a stake through one of his wrists when he grabbed him around the throat," she said. She sounded like she had a head cold with that tissue stuffed up her nose. "And then I poured holy water on it. While he was freaking out, Mill grabbed him, ripped the back of his shirt off, and we found the armor underneath."

Gregory nodded.

"Somehow, one of them managed to splash some holy water into his mouth—purely by accident, I assume," Mill went on, his eyes still closed, head back. "But as he sputtered, I managed to get a stake under his armpit. I shoved it in, and I hit the heart."

He did sit up now, and his intense, dark eyes stared right through me.

"I was trying to get up to help you when we saw Roxy dragging you down the sidewalk toward the entrance."

"Yeah, ouch. That was *not* cool of her to do," Xandra said. She reflexively touched her own head gingerly, as if feeling Roxy's fingers there herself. "She had no respect for hairstyle."

"Maybe that sunk in before she died," I said.

"But what that motorcycle chick did ..." Gregory said. "That was insane. Brutal, even."

Mill glared at me. "You really won't tell me who she is?"

I shrugged. "I guess she wanted to remain anonymous for a reason."

Mill rolled his eyes, letting his head fall back against the seat again. "She wore a helmet because it was sunup, not because she was hiding her face."

"You assume," I said. "But I'm not gonna out her. She's done a lot to protect me." Too much to just toss her identity out there. Even if Mill had more than proven himself tonight. And before.

Xandra and Gregory seemed content to discuss how crazy Iona was, and what sort of vampire she must be to ruthlessly murder another one like that. Laura was smiling a little, but it seemed ... forced. She kept looking at her hands, knitted together in her lap.

"Tough night," I told her. "It's okay to be a little shaken up. Seriously."

We pulled up to Mill's condo building, and Lockwood drove into the parking garage, finding a spot in the middle where the shadows were the darkest.

Gregory started to get out to help, but Mill shook his head.

"I'm good, kid. Thanks, though."

I stepped out, though, and walked around the car to meet him.

We stood there for a few seconds in silence. I checked out

all of the little scrapes and cuts he had, where his shirt was torn over his heart. But he was standing. He could walk.

"I'll be okay," he said. "Really."

I smiled weakly. My breathing was painful again; my ribs reminded me hotly that they were not happy with me.

"Mill ..." I said and looked up into his face.

There was something deep in that gaze that I couldn't quite pinpoint.

"I don't even know where to start," I said. "This whole thing, all of it ... was insanity. The entire night ... it could have gone wrong so many times ..."

He opened his mouth to speak, but I had to keep going.

"But it didn't," I said quickly. "And it's all because you were there, at every turn, saving me."

A smile tugged at the corner of his mouth.

"I'm literally useless," I went on. "I mean, I don't even know how to defend myself properly. I kept thinking that all night."

The gorget was still clasped in my hand.

"I guess if I'm going to keep getting dragged into your world, I'm going to have to learn how to fight, aren't I?"

Mill nodded. "Might not be a bad idea."

It was a little scary that he agreed with me. Guess I really was in deeper than I thought.

"Who do you think could teach me to fight vampires?" I asked. "I mean, I can't exactly go asking in my local dojo, right? I'd need a special trainer."

Maybe whoever taught him could teach me, too. Or maybe ...

Mill considered my words, still hunched over slightly, cradling his injury. "When I feel better ..." he said slowly, "Maybe I could."

"Really?" I asked, daring to hope. "You, uh ... seem to know what you're doing."

Mill shook his head. "I'm rusty." He laughed lightly as he looked down at himself. "Obviously."

"No, you were amazing," I said. "More than once."

A comfortable silence fell as we smiled at each other.

"I—" I started, and then cleared my throat. "I should let you get inside. Heal. Sleep."

"Yeah ..."

Mill turned slowly and started toward the elevator.

I watched him for a few seconds to make sure he was able to make it okay. And then I turned back to the car.

"Hey, Cassie?"

I wheeled around at his voice.

"Yeah?"

"Take care of yourself ... okay?"

I smirked. "I'll do my best. But just in case, keep your phone handy, all right?"

I hopped back in the car beside Xandra and watched him limp into the elevator as we pulled away.

Chapter 40

I relished the sunlight on my face as we drove away. The warm rays were like hope itself, washing away the fear of the night.

Tampa itself was starting to rise. More cars were pulling onto the road as we drove. The drive-through windows at every fast food and coffee place were packed, and people honked at one another at stoplights, late or impatient to get to their destination. And the smells! I drank them in: oil-fried foods, so inviting to my empty stomach as we passed by McDonald's; gasoline pumped by the early risers at gas stations. Even the belch of fumes as we were stuck behind a truck was wonderful. It all meant I was still here.

It all meant I was alive. That we were *all* alive.

"That was the longest night of my life," Xandra said heavily as we pulled into our neighborhood—home at last.

"Hey, Lockwood?" I said.

"Yes, Miss?" he replied, looking over at me, smiling.

"Thank you," I said, "for …"

I didn't finish. Couldn't. I was happy to have made it through, ecstatic—but it was so fresh. Talking about it in real terms, I might just break, the night's struggles finally pushing me too far.

But he understood. Eyes twinkling, he said, "You're quite welcome, Miss Cassandra."

Huh. I usually hated my full name. But from Lockwood … it sounded nice.

"What exactly happened to you tonight?" Gregory asked Xandra. The question had lingered in the back of my mind since rescuing her. I hadn't asked, none of us had. But now we were in the relative safety of our neighborhood once again, Gregory must have felt what I had: that we could begin to unspool the events of the night without Draven and/or his cronies stumbling upon us.

"Well, after you texted me, I went to the airport to try and head you off," Xandra started. "But when I got there and said who I was looking for, the security guard told me to follow him. I did. I thought something was wrong. It didn't even cross my mind that he could be a vampire, though. Who knew they'd taken over security?" She paused, thinking. "This would kind of explain why the TSA literally sucks, though.

"Anyway, I waited in this room for like two hours, totally alone. No windows, nothing. The guard even took my cell phone. When he came back, he said there was someone who wanted to see me. I thought it was you, but … turns out it was Roxy. I thought she might be one of your allies, so when she asked me who I was and why I was there, I told her."

I groaned, and she nodded.

"I know, I know. But what was I supposed to do? She hadn't attacked me, so I figured she must have been one of those nice vampires you keep talking about."

"I guess you wouldn't have been able to know that she was one of those Instaphoto vamps," I said sadly.

Xandra nodded again. "Right. Well, I guess by what I told her, she connected the dots that you weren't who you said you were." She looked pleadingly at me. "I'm really sorry, Cassie. I had no idea that you were trying to disguise yourself as a vampire. If I had known—"

"It's okay," I replied, putting a hand on her arm. "Really. It's okay. It was … another lie to blend into their world, but it's over and done with now. I'm not mad. Honest."

And this time … I was.

"I really am sorry that you got involved in all of this," I told her. "I feel so bad that you got hurt, and that you were in danger."

"I'm sorry I wasn't of more help," she said, rubbing her wrists. Like the fearful look in her eyes, and the narrow, shallow scrape on her forehead, I figured those red marks from her bonds wouldn't fade anytime in the near future. It sucked—but again: she was alive. Scarred, yes—but alive.

"Don't apologize," I said. "Seriously."

"Then let's both agree to stop apologizing," she replied. "I don't blame you for anything that happened. Okay?"

"Okay."

And she threw her arms around my neck and hugged me. We stayed that way until we pulled up in front of her house, which was first on the drop off list. She waved from her front porch as we set off back down the street.

Less than twenty-four hours ago, the two people in the back seat hardly knew me. I hardly knew them.

But now there was something that tied us all together, in a way that nothing could have before.

Lockwood pulled up beside the sidewalk and unlocked the doors to let us out.

"I am very glad that I was able to return you all to your homes this morning," he said as he lowered his window and peered out at us, still smiling. Sunlight danced across his face. Not a vampire, I guess.

"Yeah, us too," Gregory said. "Thanks for everything, Lockwood." They shook hands through the car window.

"Yes, thank you," Laura added.

He turned his bright green eyes on me. "Until we meet again, Miss Cassandra."

He tipped his hat to us, rolled up the window, and slowly made his way back down the street.

We all looked at each other, and then smiled, laughing quietly. It was weird, a heady kind of feeling, now that the danger had passed. There wasn't anything funny about standing on the sidewalk first thing in the morning, but ... we were laughing anyway.

There were these unseen threads of gratitude between all of us now. We all had jumped in, all had done something to make that night end the way it had.

"Thank you, Cassie," Laura said quietly. "Really. No one

else would have done what you did for me."

Gregory lowered his ice pack and nodded. "She's right," he said, a little ashamed. "I'm sorry that I didn't stand with you last time this all went down. Now that I know what you were up against ..."

"Don't worry about it," I said. "You more than redeemed yourself tonight. Err ... this morning, technically."

He smiled weakly. "If you ever need help in the future ..."

"I won't call you first, if that makes you feel better," I said.

Gregory's shoulders relaxed. "Thank God. Because fighting that vampire ... that was the scariest thing I've ever done. I just don't think I'm cut out for this. I don't think I'm brave. Like, not even in the neighborhood of brave. I am not brave adjacent." He swallowed hard. "Yikes."

"I wouldn't say that," I said. "Any of it."

"I thought you were really brave," Laura added.

Gregory's face flushed.

"I should let you guys get home. Get some rest," I said, watching Laura try and stifle a yawn.

We said goodbye, and I watched as they slowly made their way down the sidewalk to their houses. Gregory said something to Laura, who nodded, before they parted ways at his driveway.

I smiled.

I didn't think there was a single spot on my body that didn't ache as I dragged myself toward my house. How was it that a few hundred feet felt like a marathon?

But the sun was rising higher in the sky. The shadows were shrinking. Birds sang to one another in the branches of the trees. Mom's wind chime tinkled happily on the front porch.

I walked into the garage, hoping that I could spend my entire Saturday in bed.

I unlocked the door to the house, stepped inside and—

"*Where have you been!?*"

Mom.

Dad.

They were both standing there in the kitchen, twin, sick looks painted on their faces.

I sighed. Busted.

And there was nobody left who could save me from this.

Cassie Howell will return in

YOU CAN'T GO HOME AGAIN

Liars and Vampires
Book 3

Coming June 15, 2018!

Author's Note

Thanks for reading! If you want to know immediately when future books become available, take sixty seconds and sign up for my NEW RELEASE EMAIL ALERTS by visiting my website. I don't sell your information and I only send out emails when I have a new book out. The reason you should sign up for this is because I don't always set release dates, and even if you're following me on Facebook (robertJcrane (Author)) or Twitter (@robertJcrane), it's easy to miss my book announcements because...well, because social media is an imprecise thing.

Come join the discussion on my website:
http://www.robertjcrane.com!

Cheers,
Robert J. Crane

ACKNOWLEDGMENTS

Editing and formatting was handled expertly by Nick Bowman of nickbowman-editing.com. Sarah Barbour did another heavy editing run through, with a final proofing pass by Jo Evans. Many thanks to all of them.

Once again, the illustrious illustrator Karri Klawiter produced the cover. artbykarri.com is where you can find her amazing works.

Thanks to the great Kate Hasbrouck, my co-author (yeah, her name's not Lauren – there are reasons, we'll talk about it someday), who has been a wonderful collaborator.

And thanks as always to my family—wife, parents, in-laws and occasionally my kids—for keeping a lid on the craziness so I can do this job.

Other Works by Robert J. Crane

The Girl in the Box *and* Out of the Box
Contemporary Urban Fantasy

Alone: The Girl in the Box, Book 1
Untouched: The Girl in the Box, Book 2
Soulless: The Girl in the Box, Book 3
Family: The Girl in the Box, Book 4
Omega: The Girl in the Box, Book 5
Broken: The Girl in the Box, Book 6
Enemies: The Girl in the Box, Book 7
Legacy: The Girl in the Box, Book 8
Destiny: The Girl in the Box, Book 9
Power: The Girl in the Box, Book 10

Limitless: Out of the Box, Book 1
In the Wind: Out of the Box, Book 2
Ruthless: Out of the Box, Book 3
Grounded: Out of the Box, Book 4
Tormented: Out of the Box, Book 5
Vengeful: Out of the Box, Book 6
Sea Change: Out of the Box, Book 7
Painkiller: Out of the Box, Book 8
Masks: Out of the Box, Book 9
Prisoners: Out of the Box, Book 10
Unyielding: Out of the Box, Book 11
Hollow: Out of the Box, Book 12
Toxicity: Out of the Box, Book 13
Small Things: Out of the Box, Book 14
Hunters: Out of the Box, Book 15
Badder: Out of the Box, Book 16
Apex: Out of the Box, Book 18
Time: Out of the Box, Book 19
Driven: Out of the Box, Book 20
Remember: Out of the Box, Book 21* *(Coming August 3, 2018!)*
Hero: Out of the Box, Book 22* *(Coming October 2018!)*
Flashback: Out of the Box, Book 23* *(Coming December 2018!)*
Walk Through Fire: Out of the Box, Book 24* *(Coming in 2019!)*

World of Sanctuary
Epic Fantasy

Defender: The Sanctuary Series, Volume One
Avenger: The Sanctuary Series, Volume Two
Champion: The Sanctuary Series, Volume Three
Crusader: The Sanctuary Series, Volume Four
Sanctuary Tales, Volume One - A Short Story Collection
Thy Father's Shadow: The Sanctuary Series, Volume 4.5
Master: The Sanctuary Series, Volume Five
Fated in Darkness: The Sanctuary Series, Volume 5.5
Warlord: The Sanctuary Series, Volume Six
Heretic: The Sanctuary Series, Volume Seven
Legend: The Sanctuary Series, Volume Eight
Ghosts of Sanctuary: The Sanctuary Series, Volume Nine
Call of the Hero: The Sanctuary Series, Volume Ten* *(Coming Late 2018!)*

A Haven in Ash: Ashes of Luukessia, Volume One *(with Michael Winstone)*
A Respite From Storms: Ashes of Luukessia, Volume Two *(with Michael Winstone)*
A Home in the Hills: Ashes of Luukessia, Volume Three* *(with Michael Winstone—Coming Mid to Late 2018!)*

Southern Watch
Contemporary Urban Fantasy

Called: Southern Watch, Book 1
Depths: Southern Watch, Book 2
Corrupted: Southern Watch, Book 3
Unearthed: Southern Watch, Book 4
Legion: Southern Watch, Book 5
Starling: Southern Watch, Book 6
Forsaken: Southern Watch, Book 7* *(Coming Summer 2018!)*
Hallowed: Southern Watch, Book 8* *(Coming Late 2018/Early 2019!)*

The Shattered Dome Series

(with Nicholas J. Ambrose)
Sci-Fi

Voiceless: The Shattered Dome, Book 1
Unspeakable: The Shattered Dome, Book 2* *(Coming 2018!)*

The Mira Brand Adventures

Contemporary Urban Fantasy

The World Beneath: The Mira Brand Adventures, Book 1
The Tide of Ages: The Mira Brand Adventures, Book 2
The City of Lies: The Mira Brand Adventures, Book 3
The King of the Skies: The Mira Brand Adventures, Book 4
The Best of Us: The Mira Brand Adventures, Book 5
We Aimless Few: The Mira Brand Adventures, Book 6* *(Coming 2018!)*

Liars and Vampires

(with Lauren Harper)
Contemporary Urban Fantasy

No One Will Believe You: Liars and Vampires, Book 1
Someone Should Save Her: Liars and Vampires, Book 2
You Can't Go Home Again: Liars and Vampires, Book 3* *(Coming June 15, 2018!)*
In The Dark: Liars and Vampires, Book 4* *(Coming July 17, 2018!)*
Her Lying Days Are Done: Liars and Vampires, Book 5* *(Coming August 2018!)*
Heir of the Dog: Liars and Vampires, Book 6* *(Coming September 2018!)*
Hit You Where You Live: Liars and Vampires, Book 7* *(Coming October 2018!)*

* Forthcoming, Subject to Change

Printed in Great Britain
by Amazon